"She can be so mean," Libby whispered to me as we joined the other girls at one of the tables. I just nodded and hoped Jessica hadn't seen what had happened. My friendship with Jessica hadn't been getting anywhere as it was, and I didn't need a setback. It wasn't like Jessica was rude to me. She was very polite, but I wanted our friendship to be more than her being polite to me. I wanted her to call me at night and giggle with me on the phone for hours, the way Francie and Mary Kay and I used to do. So that afternoon, to make myself feel better, I gave her my phone number, in case she decided to call.

"Thank you Cathy," Jessica said, as she examined the piece of paper I'd handed her. "But if this is your phone number, you already gave it to me."

"I did?" I squeaked. I'd developed an awful tendency to squeak around Jessica. I never squeaked anywhere else.

"Last week," she said, and smiled kindly at me. "Thank you, but I really don't need two copies." She handed back the neatly folded piece of paper.

Other Apple paperbacks you will enjoy:

Kid Power
   by Susan Beth Pfeffer
Starting with Melodie
   by Susan Beth Pfeffer
Adorable Sunday
   by Marlene Fanta Shyer
A Season of Secrets
   by Alison Cragin Herzig
   and Jane Lawrence Mali
Starstruck
   by Marisa Gioffre
The Trouble with Soap
   by Margery Cuyler.

Truth or Dare

Susan Beth Pfeffer

AN
APPLE®
PAPERBACK

SCHOLASTIC INC.
New York Toronto London Auckland Sydney

ISBN 0-590-41104-7

12 11 10 9 8 7 6 5 4 3 2   8 9/8 0 1/9

Printed in the U.S.A.   01

Truth or Dare

TO PAM MATHER-CATHY
For this summer, and better ones

Chapter 1

When your world has come to an absolute end, it's hard to believe that people expect you to go on. In less than six months, my two best friends and my favorite brother had practically vanished from my life, and I was still expected to go to school.

Language arts class had just started, but already I was bored and miserable. I only hoped I wouldn't feel this way for the rest of the school year. We were only on day one; that left an awful lot of time to be bored and miserable. And I wanted to die from loneliness.

I used to like school. Not studying or homework, but everything else about school was okay. Writing compositions had always been one of my favorite things to do too, and now all I could do was stare at Mr. Flynn, my language arts teacher, and wonder how such an insensitive person ever got to teach sixth graders.

"I've never taught sixth graders before," he said, almost answering my question. "So we're going to have to learn together."

Comments like that don't build confidence. My world had come to an absolute end, and I wasn't even going to have a teacher who knew what he was doing. For this my parents paid taxes?

"Very well then," Mr. Flynn said, although nothing seemed very well at all, and I knew he knew it. "Let's start the school year with a composition. I always say writing is the best form of communication, except for conversation."

"And sex," one of the boys muttered. I was close enough to hear him and embarrassed enough to blush. If this was what junior high was going to be like, no wonder Mary Kay's parents insisted she go to parochial school. No wonder Francie's mother left town. No wonder my world had shattered.

Actually Francie's mother had decided she and Francie were going to move before it was announced that all the sixth graders were going to go to the junior high. Not that she would have approved. As far as I could figure out, none of the parents of kids who'd be in the sixth grade approved, but somehow the measure got passed.

"It has to do with the school budget," my mother tried explaining to me. "And population shifts."

Even then I scowled, and I didn't know Mary Kay would be going to St. Theresa's.

"You see, the elementary schools are overcrowded," Mom continued. "And the high school doesn't have enough students. So, if they move all the sixth graders to the junior high, then the ninth graders can go to the high school. The elementary schools won't be overcrowded anymore, and the high school will be full again, and the junior high will remain about the same. It's really very practical."

I guess if Francie and Mary Kay had started junior high with me, then I wouldn't have hated it so much. But Francie hadn't even finished fifth grade with us. She and her mother had left by April, when her mother got a great new job in Chicago. And that had just left Mary Kay and me to be best friends, and now I didn't have Mary Kay, either. Mary Kay's parents had gotten hysterical at the thought of her going to junior high.

"She's only ten," her mother pointed out to my mother. "Mary Kay has always been the youngest in her class. I don't think it's right for a ten-year-old to be in junior high school."

"It's only a building," my mom said.

"I only wish that were true," Mary Kay's mother said. "But I remember junior high. It isn't just a building. It's an entire way of life."

When I realized I was going to be in junior high without my two best friends, I cried for a solid week. Everyone in my family tried to comfort me, but it didn't work.

"You can see Mary Kay anytime you want," Dad pointed out. "She isn't leaving town."

"When you go to a different school, you might as well live in a different world," I said.

"You and Francie can write to each other," Mom said. "You love writing letters."

"But it won't be nearly the same as having her with me," I said. "And Francie writes terrible letters."

"You can meet exciting new people," my sister Andrea said long-distance from Boston. "Just think of this as an opportunity to expand your horizons."

"I liked my horizons," I said, "just the way they were."

"You place too much importance on friends," my brother Paul said. "Friends are important, but they're not everything. If there were only something that really interested you, the way dance interests me."

"But there isn't," I said. Paul dances. Paul's always danced, and it's the only thing that's ever interested him. It's made him a very boring person. I guess other dancers think he's interesting, but to anybody who doesn't think the world begins and ends with the ballet, Paul is about as dull as a person can be. Just seeing how boring Paul is has kept me from developing any hobbies. I once almost got interested in stamp collecting, but when I thought about only talking about stamps, and talking with people who collect stamps, and not having any friends who didn't collect stamps also, I really panicked. For the longest time I didn't dare look at an envelope.

"I don't have any advice for you," my brother Mark said. "It's going to be very rough. But I know you'll make it through and make new friends, and things will be okay for you again."

I sat there in language arts, trying to pay attention to what Mr. Flynn was saying, but just thinking about what Mark had said made me want to start crying all over again. What a way to start junior high, though, sobbing like some kindergartener.

But I missed Mark so much, and he'd only been gone a week. He started college in North Carolina, where he is a physical therapy major. That's the sort of person Mark is. He helps people; he cares about them. He's always cared about me, and while I didn't miss him as much as Francie and Mary Kay put together, I certainly missed him more than either one of them alone.

Mark may have been seven years older than me, but he always let me tag along and do stuff with him. I was the mascot on his junior high soccer team. He played horsy with me all the time when I was little, and as I got older he always had time to help me with my homework. Not like Andrea, who started college when I was seven, so I hardly knew her. Or Paul, who's three years older than me, but is always practicing or at ballet class or generally unaware that there's more to life than second position.

"All right, class," Mr. Flynn was saying when I started paying attention again. "I know this is hokey, but it's a good way for us to get to know one another. I want every one of you to write just a paragraph or two about what you did during your summer vacation."

Everyone in the class groaned. I'd never heard twenty-eight groans at once before. It was pretty impressive.

"Come on, guys," Mr. Flynn said. "One paragraph isn't going to kill you."

"That's what you think," Billy Thompson said. I knew him from elementary school. Actually I knew about a third of the kids in the class, but I didn't know any of them really well. The person I knew best was Libby Katz, who'd been a pretty good friend up until third grade, when Francie started at our school. Libby and Francie didn't get along, and I ended up being best friends with Francie. Libby had other friends, so I didn't feel so bad that we'd stopped being friends.

"Get going," Mr. Flynn said. "And you'd better put something decent down on paper, because I intend to call on as many of you as I can fit in."

Absolutely nothing had happened to me during summer vacation except the destruction of my entire world, but that wasn't anything I wanted to write about. I chewed on my pencil for a moment or two, trying to think if anything else had happened that was worth writing about.

"During the summer, I watched a lot of TV."

It was true, but it wasn't a paragraph, and it probably wasn't something Mr. Flynn would want to hear.

"During the summer, I was very bored all the time."

Good, not great.

"During the summer, my best friend's parents decided to send her to parochial school, so she wouldn't be stuck here."

Actually that happened more to Mary Kay and her parents than it did to me. And Mr. Flynn might be offended by it. So I concentrated some more, and then I remembered we'd all taken a vacation together. Paul had complained about it, because it meant he missed practicing, and I hadn't much wanted to go because I was so busy crying, but Mom and Dad insisted.

"During the summer, my family went on a trip to Boston to visit my sister, Andrea, who went to college there. She has an apartment but we stayed at a motel."

The reason we stayed at a motel was because Andrea lives with her boyfriend, Harvey, and Dad hates Harvey. As far as I know, Harvey is the only person my father really hates, except for some politicians he's never met, but he sure does hate

8

Harvey. Harvey inherited lots of money from his grandparents, but he looks kind of sleazy. He has this little thin mustache that he's always bragging about, and he's already losing his hair. He met Andrea two years ago, and she moved in with him last year, and Dad got really hysterical then. Fortunately the apartment wasn't big enough for Mom, Dad, Mark, Paul, and me as well as Harvey and Andrea, so it made sense for us to stay in a motel.

"We saw lots of interesting stuff in Boston," I wrote. "We saw where Paul Revere rode. And we went to Concord and saw Walden Pond where somebody famous lived." I wished I could remember just who. "And we ate out every night except for when Andrea cooked for us." Andrea is a terrible cook, so eating out was like staying at the motel, more expensive but definitely necessary. "My whole family had a good time and I learned many interesting things."

I checked my paragraph over, and it looked okay to me. I'd left out all the interesting stuff about Harvey, but there are some things you just don't write about in junior high. I may have only been in junior high for three hours, but I knew that much.

"Very well," Mr. Flynn said. "Any

volunteers? Does anyone want to read his or her composition?"

Of course nobody volunteered.

"Then I'll pick and choose," he said. "You," he said, and pointed to a boy in the second row. "Ralph Smith, why don't we start with you."

"Do I have to stand up?" Ralph asked.

"Absolutely not," Mr. Flynn said.

"Okay," Ralph said. "During the summer I read a lot of comic books and watched TV."

"Is that it?" Mr. Flynn asked.

"That's all I did," Ralph said.

"Fine," Mr. Flynn said. "Pithy even."

Ralph smirked. I had to admit I was jealous. If I'd known that was all there was to it, I would have written the same thing, and left out Paul Revere and Walden Pond.

"All right then," Mr. Flynn said. "You, next. Jessica Green."

We all looked around to see who Jessica Green would be. She was sitting two seats away from me, so I got to look at her really carefully.

She had beautiful hair, reddish brown and lots of it. Her nose was small and it actually tipped up like a model's. She was wearing a shirt that looked like the kind that got pressed, and some sort of skirt that I couldn't see too well. She was definitely the prettiest girl in our class, and probably in the entire junior high. I've always wanted hair that looked like that.

"I spent my summer vacation in Europe," she read out loud. "My father took my mother and me to France, England, and Italy. We saw the Eiffel Tower, the Crown Jewels, and the Vatican. My favorite part was seeing the *Mona Lisa*, a famous painting by Leonardo da Vinci. That was at the Louvre, a museum in Paris. We also got to meet many interesting European families, and we stayed at their homes. I hope to go back to Europe someday and see the *Mona Lisa* again."

"Well," Mr. Flynn said. "Very impressive, Jessica. A lot more interesting than reading comic books and watching TV, I'd imagine."

Jessica smiled. She had the whitest teeth I'd ever seen. They were so white it looked like she'd painted them.

Mr. Flynn called on other kids then, but he didn't call on me, and I didn't listen very hard. Mark had said I'd make new friends, and he was right, the way he always was. And I knew who my first new friend would be.

All I had to figure out was how to get Jessica Green to like me half as much as I already liked her.

Chapter 2

Jessica and I had language arts, social studies, and math together. We already had our seats for language arts and math, but I made a point of sitting next to her in social studies. She didn't seem to mind, but she didn't smile at me or say hello or anything. Of course I wanted her to, but I knew it would take time before we really became friends.

So at lunch the second day of school I checked to see who Jessica was eating with. I was really happy to see she was with Libby, especially since I didn't know the other girls Jessica was with. But as long as she was with Libby, I figured it was okay to go to her table and act pleased to see Libby. Jessica would never guess I was really there because of her.

"Hi, Cathy," Libby said as soon as she saw me. She smiled and made me feel like it was normal for me to be joining her for lunch.

"Hi, Libby," I said, balancing my books and my tray. "Can I join you?"

"Sure," she replied, and cleared off a spot next to her at the table. "Sit down."

So I did. Libby took a bite out of her sandwich, so I guessed she'd decided she'd done enough for me. "My name is Cathy," I said. "I went to South Street School."

"I'm Michelle," one of the other girls said. "I'm from Montgomery."

"So am I," Jessica said, with a friendly smile. "This is Amy, and she went there too."

"I guess you're all friends from there then," I said.

"Since first grade," Michelle said. "Are you and Libby old friends?"

I nodded, suddenly feeling terrible that Libby and I hadn't been close since third grade. But Libby didn't say anything about that.

"I really liked your composition yesterday," I said to Jessica. "We're in language arts together."

"I thought you looked familiar," she said. "Do we have any other classes together?"

I wished I'd made more of an impression on her, but at least she didn't hate me. "A couple," I said. "Europe really sounded great."

"It was fun," Jessica said. "Except the food was terrible. Mom and Dad made us eat at all the foreign restaurants. I didn't have a single hamburger or slice of pizza the entire time I was there."

"Yuck," Amy said. "I'd die without pizza.

"I almost did," Jessica said. "But the rest of it was really great."

"Was the *Mona Lisa* as wonderful as you said?" I asked.

Jessica shrugged her shoulders. "It was okay," she said. "There was a big crowd around it, so it was kind of hard to really see it. And it wasn't very big. I always figured a painting that famous had to be really big. There were other paintings I liked more, but I figured Mr. Flynn had probably heard of the *Mona Lisa*, and I didn't want to make him feel dumb. Actually I liked the Crown Jewels best."

"I went to Disneyworld last year," Michelle said. "That was neat."

"I've never been anywhere," Libby said. "Unless you count Minnesota."

"You've been to Minnesota?" I asked. "Why?"

"My grandmother lives there," Libby said. "We go every summer to see her. It's really kind of pretty there. You can pick blueberries and there are lots of cows."

"Do they have pizza there?" Amy asked.

Libby laughed. "Lots," she said. "And plenty of hamburgers."

"Then it's probably about as good as Europe," Jessica said. "You don't have the Crown Jewels, but you do have good food."

"I went to Boston last summer," I said. Since Mr. Flynn hadn't gotten around to calling on me to read my composition, nobody knew about my trip to Boston. It sure wasn't Europe, but it was all I had, except a trip to Washington, D.C. three years ago.

"I've been to Boston," Amy said. "My brother went to college in Boston, and we all went there for his graduation."

"Really?" I asked. "My sister went to college there too. Maybe they went to the same school."

"Boston University," Amy said. "He graduated two years ago."

"Andrea went to Northeastern," I said. "And she graduated in June. We were all supposed to go to her graduation, but Dad had a big meeting, and I got sick, and my brother Paul . . . well, he was busy." I decided fast not to mention Paul's dancing. Some people thought it was weird for a boy to dance, so I'm usually pretty careful about whom I tell. "My mom got time off from work though and she went with my other brother Mark. And then in the summer we all went to visit Andrea and her boyfriend, Harvey."

"My brother doesn't have a girl friend," Amy said. "Or if he does, he sure isn't telling us. He doesn't tell us a lot of stuff though, so maybe he's even married."

"I wish I had an older brother," Libby said.

"You can have mine," Amy said. "No one in my family would miss him."

"Amy's brother is actually pretty cute," Jessica said.

"You know who else is cute?" Michelle said. "Bobby Phillips."

"You think so?" I said. Bobby and I had been in school together since first grade and I never thought of him as cute. Of course I was only just starting to notice that boys were cute at all.

"Absolutely," Michelle said. "I love hair that color."

I thought hard to remember Bobby's hair color. It was brown, it seemed to me, not that different from Michelle's color. Maybe he just looked better to girls who came from Montgomery.

"All Michelle ever talks about is boys," Amy said.

"All you ever talk about is pizza," Michelle said.

Jessica laughed, so I laughed too. Libby just kept eating her sandwich. "Amy and Michelle are always fighting about something," Jessica told me.

I knew this was an important moment. Jessica was telling me something so I'd understand her friends better. That must mean she likes me too, I thought.

"I love my mother, but she makes terrible sandwiches," Libby declared, taking one final bite. "All jelly and never enough peanut butter."

"Couldn't you make your own sandwiches?" I asked. "I always make my own."

"That's not how it works in my family," Libby said. "Mom does the cooking, and I do the dishes. That's because Mom hates doing the dishes."

"We take turns in my family," I said. "Except my brother Paul is always skipping his turn." Now that Mark was gone, there would be one less person doing the dishes, I realized. Another reason to miss Mark.

"How old is Paul?" Michelle asked.

"He's fourteen," I said.

"Uhm," Michelle said. "Is he cute?"

"I don't know," I said. "He's my brother."

"Maybe you could invite us over to meet him," Michelle said. "And we could see for ourselves. Fourteen is such a sexy age."

"Eighty is a sexy age as far as Michelle is concerned," Amy said.

This time we all laughed. "Sure I can bring you over," I said. "Paul's pretty busy, but there's bound to be sometime when he's around and you all can meet him."

"That would be fun," Jessica said. "We'll have to do that sometime, Katie."

"Cathy," I said, wondering if maybe I should change my name to Katie. It did have a nice sound to it.

"Cathy," Jessica said, and smiled right at me. She had the most beautiful smile I'd ever seen. I'll bet she never had a cavity a day in her life. "I'm sorry. I'm terrible at names."

"That's okay," I said. "You don't know me, that's all."

"Katie's a nice name too," Amy said. "But Cathy's nicer."

"More feminine," Michelle said.

"We all have pretty names," Amy said. "Except maybe Libby."

I was surprised by what Amy said. It seemed kind of mean to me.

"I like Libby," Libby said sharply. "Besides, my real name is Elizabeth, so I can change my nickname anytime I want. You're going to be Amy the rest of your life."

"I'd rather be Amy than Libby," Amy said.

"I'd rather be Melinda," Michelle said. "I think Melinda is the most beautiful name in the world."

"I think we'd better clear the table and get going," Jessica said. "That's what I think."

It was amazing. As soon as she said it, we all started clearing the table. Jessica had the most amazing leadership abilities, just the kind teachers were always talking about.

"I'll see you later," I said to her. "We still have social studies together."

"We do?" she asked. "That'll be nice."

"It sure will," I said, and then I felt really dumb. But Jessica had already wandered off with Amy and Michelle before I had a chance to explain just what I meant. Not that I was sure just what it was I did mean. But whatever I meant, I hadn't meant it to sound that dumb.

"Jessica's really nice," I said to Libby as we started walking out of the cafeteria.

"I like her," Libby said. "Not everybody does, but I do."

"What don't people like about her?" I asked.

"I'll tell you after school," she said. "I don't think it's right to talk about somebody in school, do you?"

I'd never given it any thought. "You're right," I said. "Somebody might overhear."

"Exactly," Libby said. "You live kind of near me anyway, don't you?"

"Mulberry Street," I said.

"I'm on Oak," she said. "We can walk home together, like we used to."

"Fine," I said, although I would rather have walked home with Jessica. Not that she asked me. Not that I even knew where Jessica lived. Libby would just have to do.

The rest of the school day passed pretty quickly. In social studies Jessica noticed that I was sitting next to her, and she smiled at me and said hi. I noticed that Amy and Michelle were both in my gym class, so when we picked teams, I made sure to be on theirs, and we played soccer together. Libby was in my science class and even though we didn't sit near each other, she passed a note over to me that said, "Meet me after school." All of which made junior high a lot nicer than it had been the day before.

Even so, I was impatient for the school day to end, so Libby and I could talk. I had study hall last period, and I thought it would never end. I pretended to do my math homework, and I tried looking at my social studies textbook, but mostly I doodled and thought about how I'd made these four terrific friends in just one day. I decided I'd write to Francie just as soon as I got home to let her know. I thought about calling Mary Kay to tell her, but I thought that might make her feel bad. If she didn't have to go to St. Theresa's then she'd be in the junior high with me making the same terrific friends. I'd tell Mary Kay, but only when I was sure she'd made new friends too.

Eventually the school bell rang, and we all jumped up and ran to our lockers to get our stuff. I had no trouble spotting Libby outside and we started walking home together like it was the most normal thing in the world.

"Jessica and Amy and Michelle said they were going to Comptons," Libby declared, as we started our walk. "Michelle said she heard that all the cutest boys hang out there, and Amy said she heard they made the best ice-cream cones there, so they figured they'd try it."

"My brother Mark used to get stuff there

when he was in junior high," I said. "He said Mrs. Compton was really mean to the kids."

"She sure is," Libby said. "I went there once with my friend Megan, and Mrs. Compton practically kicked us out for no reason."

"I'd like to try her ice cream though," I said. "I love ice cream."

"The ice cream is wonderful," Libby said.

"Well, if it has good food and cute boys then both Amy and Michelle will be happy," I said. "I guess Mrs. Compton won't be too bad then."

"She'll probably like Jessica," Libby said. "Some kids think Jessica is stuck up, but grown-ups always like Jessica. Mom says that's because Jessica has really great manners."

"Good manners are important," I said. I vaguely remembered my mother screaming that at us once.

"Sure they are," Libby said. "They make grown-ups like you."

"That's important too," I said. And then all of a sudden I realized what Libby had said. Her mother knew Jessica. Libby must know her really well then. I could ask her all kinds of things about Jessica. "How do

you think Jessica got her great manners?"
I asked for starters.

"My mom says Jessica's mom has lovely
manners and that's why Jessica has them,"
Libby replied. "Their house is always spotless too."

I'd never seen a spotless house, but I
could imagine what one looked like. It
seemed right that Jessica lived in a spotless
house and had a mother with great
manners.

"Is she rich?" I asked. "She acts like
she's rich."

"I guess so," Libby said. "Jessica's
father is a big doctor in New York. He has
lots of famous patients."

"Wow," I said. "I bet that's why their
house is so spotless. Doctors are used to
having things really clean."

"My father's a doctor too," Libby said.
"But he doesn't mind a little clutter. He
says he likes it."

A little clutter was almost as exciting
to me as spotless. My mother says if you
live in a house with less than two closets
per person you should expect a total mess.
There are six of us and six closets and a
total mess.

"Is that how you know Jessica?" I asked.
"Because your fathers are both doctors?"

Libby laughed. "Just the opposite," she said. "My mom and Jessica's went to college together. They ran into each other years ago, and they've been friends ever since. They were always bringing us over to play with each other."

"So she's your best friend?" I asked.

"No," Libby said. "I don't really have a best friend right now."

"Why not?" I asked.

"Well, I was good friends with Megan Jones, but we started fighting all the time last year," Libby said. "We used to like to do all the same stuff, but then all of a sudden she liked video games and I didn't like them that much, and we'd fight about what we should do. I'd want to go to the movies, and she'd want to go to the arcade, and it wasn't fun anymore."

"I had two best friends," I said. "But one of them moved last year and the other one is going to St. Theresa's now."

"It's rough," Libby said. "When you have a best friend you can count on her to do all the fun stuff with. And she's someone to talk to about the important stuff."

"And study with," I said, thinking about how often Francie and Mary Kay and I had studied for tests together. "And have sleepovers with and giggle with."

"Mom says I'll be making new friends

this year," Libby said. "She says it's perfectly normal to make new friends as you get older. Especially in junior high."

"My brother Mark said the same thing," I said.

"Jessica's been really nice about letting me hang out with her and Amy and Michelle," Libby continued. "But they're her friends, you know. That's why I was glad you joined us at lunch."

"I was glad you made room for me," I replied. "It's like we're old friends and new friends at the same time."

"I like that," Libby said, and smiled at me.

I smiled back. Old friends and new friends and new old friends. With Jessica as my best friend, everything would turn out just fine.

Chapter 3

The next day at lunchtime, I stood in the cafeteria, holding my tray, hoping someone at Jessica's table would notice me and invite me over. Sure enough, Libby spotted me and waved. I would have preferred it if Jessica had seen me, but I was willing to settle for Libby. At least it was a start.

"Hi, everyone," I said, feeling kind of shy. "Mind if I join you?"

"Not at all," Jessica said. "There's an extra chair here just for you, Cathy." She smiled brightly at me.

She remembered my name! She might even have saved a chair for me. Life really was getting better and better.

"We were just talking about Jessica's plans for winter vacation," Amy said. "They sound great."

"You already have plans for December?" I asked.

"My parents like to make plans early for things," Jessica replied. "My mother always says it's better to plan ahead and then make changes than not to make your plans until it's too late."

"Jessica is going to California," Michelle said. "Again."

"Jessica's been to California a thousand times," Amy said.

"More," Michelle said. "I'm so jealous. Do you know how many great-looking boys there are in California?"

"No," Libby said. "How many are there, Michelle?"

"Millions," Michelle answered. "At least."

"She gets to go to Disneyland too," Amy said. "I've always wanted to go to Disneyland."

"It is fun," Jessica said. "I go with my cousins. We only go to California because my uncle lives there."

"Her uncle is a big-shot director," Michelle said. "And he knows all the big stars, and he has parties for them whenever Jessica's family is out there, and Jessica gets to meet everybody."

"I don't meet everybody," Jessica said. "But I do get to meet some of my favorite stars. And sometimes someone'll take my picture with them. I really enjoy that."

"I'll bet," I said. "I've never met any-body famous."

"Some of them can be really obnoxious," Jessica declared. "Especially if they've been drinking. But most of them are very friendly. I love going to California."

"Tell Cathy about your uncle's house," Amy said. "That house sounds so wonder-ful."

"He lives in Beverly Hills," Jessica said. "With his new wife and their kids. I guess she isn't really his new wife anymore, but that's what my father calls her because my uncle was married once before, and my father liked his first wife better."

"Tell us about the house," Amy insisted. "Enough about your uncle's wives."

Jessica laughed. "Amy loves to hear about the house," she explained to me. "I have to tell her about it every time I come back from California."

"I just wish I got to visit people with houses like that," Amy said. "You should see the pictures of it."

"It's very big," Jessica said. "I guess there are eight bedrooms, and each one has a bath, and there's a living room and dining room and all that. It's very Spanish looking."

"It has a pool," Amy said impatiently. "And a pool house with separate rooms for the men and women to change in. And a tennis court. They have their own tennis court. Can you imagine?"

"That's amazing," I said. "I've never seen a house like that, except on TV."

"Sometimes if it's really hot when we're there, we go swimming in December," Jessica said. "I like that best of all."

"She comes back with a suntan," Michelle said. "All my family ever does is go to my grandparents' house in New Jersey. Nobody ever got a suntan in New Jersey. Not even in the summertime."

"Do you travel much?" Jessica asked me. "You must find all this talk about my family really boring."

"No, I don't," I said, a little more loudly than I'd intended. "It's hard for my family to plan vacations together because my parents both work, and they have to get time off at the same time, and that's hard for them sometimes. We did go to Boston, but I already told you about that."

"I've never been to Boston," Jessica said. "I'll bet it's very nice."

"Beverly Hills sounds nicer," I said.

"My family only goes to Minnesota in the summer," Libby said. "If you go in the winter lots of times you can get snowed in until springtime."

"I'd die if I got snowed in in New

Jersey," Michelle said. "I think there's a law against cute boys living in New Jersey."

"Just as long as there's food, I don't care where I am," Amy said. "But I guess if I had to choose between Beverly Hills and New Jersey, I'd pick Beverly Hills."

"I like it here," Libby said. "I'd pick New York."

"That wasn't the choice," Amy said. "It was between New Jersey and Beverly Hills."

"Libby's family came with mine a couple of years ago," Jessica said. "They stayed at a hotel, but we did stuff together all the time. Libby and I had a great time."

I stared at Libby. I couldn't believe she'd been in California with Jessica and hadn't even thought it worth mentioning. I would have been thrilled just going to New Jersey with Jessica. She probably knew millions of famous people even there.

"Is there any place you'd like to go, Cathy?" Jessica asked me. I loved how she was trying to draw me into the conversation. I had to think hard, though, to come up with any place glamorous enough to impress her.

"Bolivia," I finally said.

Jessica's eyes opened wide. "Bolivia?" she asked. "Why there?"

I had done a paper on Bolivia the year before, but that seemed like a dumb reason. I tried to remember what I'd said in my paper that would be a good reason to want to go to Bolivia, and finally I remembered the Andes.

"The Andes," I said. "They're a giant mountain range. I'd really love to see the Andes."

"What an interesting place to want to go," Jessica said. "I'm impressed."

I had impressed Jessica. Without even meaning to. Thank goodness I had remembered the Andes.

"How's your sandwich today, Libby?" Amy asked. "Better than yesterday's?"

"Much," Libby said. "I bought it here."

We all laughed. I loved laughing with them. It made me feel like part of a crowd, the way I used to feel with Francie and Mary Kay. I kept that warm happy feeling through the rest of lunch, and during my afternoon classes, and straight through my walk home. I didn't see Libby after school, so I walked home alone, but it still felt good.

As soon as I got in, I started writing to Mark to tell him about my new friends, and about Jessica in particular. She was so exciting and friendly and modest. I'd noticed how she never bragged about herself unless

Amy or Michelle made her. And whenever the conversation would be about her for too long, she's change the subject by asking somebody a question. Most of the time it was me. I hadn't been able to keep count of how often she'd smiled at me, it was so many times. She was definitely the most wonderful friend I'd ever had, and I was just very sorry Mark wouldn't get to meet her until Thanksgiving.

I was in the middle of telling him all about how interested Jessica was in Bolivia, when the doorbell rang. Paul wasn't home yet, so I figured it was probably for me.

I was right. It was Mary Kay. Except that she was dressed in her parochial school uniform, and for a moment I really didn't recognize her. She looked so strange in a white blouse and blue-and-gray-plaid jumper.

"Aren't you going to ask me in?" she said to me, as I gawked at her.

"Sure," I replied. "Sorry, Mary Kay. I just wasn't expecting to see you."

"I came over after school," she said. "I told my mother I would. Isn't this uniform awful?"

"It is pretty bad," I agreed.

"It's hot too," Mary Kay said. We walked into the living room together and sat down on the sofa. "I hate parochial school," she told me. "I hate everything about it. I hate the teachers and the kids and the uniform. My parents say I'll just have to adjust, but I never will. I'm going to hate it forever. How's junior high?"

"It's okay," I said. "I miss you, though."

"I miss you too," Mary Kay said. "And I miss Francie, and I miss my old life. I've cried every night this week. I try to make sure to do it when my parents will hear me, but sometimes I don't even care. The TV set'll be on, and I'll cry anyway. I am the most miserable person who ever lived."

"It'll get better," I said. "I was pretty miserable just two days ago, when school started, and already I feel a lot better about things."

"Yeah?" Mary Kay said. "Why?"

"No real reason," I said. "I've just been meeting interesting people. I've been expanding my horizons."

"I guess I've been expanding mine too," Mary Kay said. "New rotten school, new rotten teachers, new rotten students. New rotten horizons."

I giggled. Mary Kay looked angry for a moment, but then she smiled at me. "I sound awful, don't I?" she said.

"You sound unhappy," I said.

"I just hate it so much," she said. "And

I always will, and I miss going to school with you. We'll still be friends though, won't we, Cathy? Just because we're going to different schools now doesn't mean we can't still be best friends, does it?"

"No, of course not," I said, but I felt uneasy saying it. Mary Kay looked so strange in her uniform. She didn't look like the Mary Kay I had known forever. And she wasn't nearly as pretty or interesting as Jessica. I wasn't sure she'd even been to New Jersey, let alone Beverly Hills or Europe.

"I've written to Francie every night this week. She doesn't like it much in Chicago."

"She told me that too," I said.

"I guess none of us are very happy then," Mary Kay said. "That's pretty funny. Last year we were all so happy together, and now we're all miserable."

I wasn't feeling all that miserable myself, but I didn't want to make Mary Kay feel worse by telling her that. So I tried to look equally miserable. It wasn't easy.

Mary Kay stared at me and then she giggled. "Things aren't that bad," she said. "Look, as long as I'm here, why don't we try to enjoy ourselves? We can listen to records, can't we?"

"Sure," I said. "I don't have anything new, though."

"That's okay," Mary Kay said. "Right now I think I'd rather listen to something I already know. It'll feel more normal."

So I went to the record cabinet and found something familiar for us to listen to. I hoped it would make Mary Kay feel better. But I didn't think it would help me any. And I wasn't all that sure I wanted things to stay familiar. I was starting to enjoy my new horizons, even if Mary Kay hated hers.

Chapter 4

We were sitting at the dinner table, listening to Paul discuss his next dance recital when the doorbell rang.

"I'll get it," I said, eager to get away from the table. Paul may not bore my parents, but he sure puts me to sleep.

I made it to the front door in record time and opened it equally fast. Any interruption would be a welcome one. But I certainly wasn't expecting the interruption I found standing there.

"Pumpkin!" my big sister Andrea shouted, and then she hugged me so hard I gave up breathing. "I'm home!"

"Andrea," I managed to gasp out.

"Who is it, Cathy?" my mother called to me from the dining room.

"It's me, Mom," Andrea shouted, and before I knew it, she'd swept her bags, her body, and me into the living room. It wasn't half a second before Mom and Dad joined us in there and Andrea was hugging them. Paul took a little longer (for a dancer, he moves awfully slowly), but Andrea gave him a hug too, and then she hugged all of us again. "I'm home for good," she announced, and plopped down in the best chair in the living room as though to prove it.

"What do you mean, dear?" Mom asked. "I thought you and Harvey. . . ."

"Don't even mention that creep Harvey to me," Andrea said. "What a turkey. I can't imagine how I put up with him for as long as I did. Every day a misery, every thought a heartache. What a fool I was."

"I certainly never liked him," Dad said. I saw Mom take a little swipe at him.

"Did the two of you have a fight, Andrea?" Mom asked.

"Nothing that simple, Mom," Andrea replied. "Nothing that cut and dried. Nothing that mundane. He was poisoning me, Mom, with his lies and half-truths and myths."

"Myths?" Dad asked.

"Psychic myths, Dad," Andrea said. "Of course since you're a man you probably believe those same myths. Poor Mom."

Dad looked stunned. Paul raised his eyebrows at me. I stared at Mom to see what Dad's myths had done to her.

"Don't worry, Mom," Andrea said. "Or you either, Dad. I'm not going to try to show either of you the errors of your ways. You're both old now, and not about to change. You've made your peace with your failures."

"Thank you, Andrea," Dad said. "I'm greatly relieved to hear it. How long do you intend to say with us?"

"Forever," Andrea said. "Or at least until I recover my psychic energies. That creep Harvey came close to destroying me, and it may take me awhile to recover the real Andrea."

"You mean you're a fake Andrea?" I asked.

"Poor child," Andrea said, focusing her attention on me. "Victimized already by the male establishment. Don't worry, pumpkin. Your big sister is here to help you avoid the mistakes that they'll be urging you to make. Andrea is here, sweetie, and everything will be all right from now on."

"Just how long do you think it will take you to recover your psychic energies?" Mom asked. "Not that we aren't delighted to have you for as long as you'd like, darling."

"I have to reevaluate my entire life," Andrea said. "Free from the influence of you know who. For the past two years every move I've made, I've made under his spiteful influence. I never wanted to be a Russian literature major. He made me. He thought it would sound good to his friends if he could tell them that was what his girl friend was majoring in. I wanted a degree in something useful, something I could get a job with, build a career out of. But no. For him it was Tolstoy or nothing. I hate Tolstoy."

"So you're thinking of graduate school?" Mom asked.

"It's a possibility," Andrea said. "Of course the grants and loans situation is a little bleak right now. I'm also thinking of becoming a truck driver. I love driving, you know, and I love diners, and long lonely nights on endless highways. You can get fabulous material for novels from driving a truck."

"There is that," Dad said. "Well, those are certainly interesting possibilities, Andrea. If you don't mind my masculine point of view."

"I welcome it," Andrea said. "I welcome all the feedback all of you are going to be giving me the next few months."

"Months," Dad said.

"It's September now," Andrea said. "And it's going to take me at least two months to regain my psychic energies and figure out what I want to do with my life. Probably longer, but we'll say two months just for the sake of argument. And that brings us to November, and there's no point looking for a job between Thanksgiving and New Year's, because nobody quits a job then, and you'd have to be a real Scrooge to fire somebody at that time of year. I'll bet you've never fired anybody between Thanksgiving and New Year's, have you, Dad?"

"I did once," Dad admitted. "But he was an embezzler."

"And I'll bet you felt terrible having to do it," Andrea said. "So that brings us to January, which is a terrible month to hunt for a job, because of the snow and the cold weather."

"February's like that too," Dad said.

"I know," Andrea said. "Believe me, I just spent four years in Boston. I have a graduate degree in winters. But even so, I'll probably start looking around for a job after New Year's. I doubt I'll find anything just then because the people who hire are always out with the flu in the winter, but it won't hurt to start looking, to see what's available. Probably nothing the way the economy is, but it won't hurt to look. If I'm lucky, I'll find something in the next six months. Something that will make me truly content. Something that will make the two of you proud of me. I know how important that is to you, Mom and Dad, and I don't intend to disappoint you again."

"That's very nice of you, dear," Mom said. She looked like her entire summer tan had vanished in just ten minutes.

"Meanwhile I'll just take back my old bedroom and you'll hardly even know I'm here," Andrea said. "I'll just tiptoe around and search for my soul in quiet."

"You can't take back your bedroom," Paul said. "That's the family room now."

"It was my bedroom first, Paul," Andrea said. "Of course I can take it back."

"But I practice there," Paul said. "My equipment's there."

"The TV's there too," I said.

"You can move all that junk out," Andrea said. "Not that your dance equipment is junk, Paul. Of course it isn't. I'm so proud of you dancing the ballet. I bragged about you to all my friends. It used to drive that creep Harvey crazy the way I'd go on and on about you. You do still dance, don't you, Paul?"

"I sure do," he said. "In the family room."

"Well, now you'll dance in the living room where we can all see you," Andrea said. "I'll love watching you practice. Ballet is so sexy on a man."

I looked at Paul to see if he was the least bit sexy. Not that I could see.

"The closet in that room is filled with things," Mom said. "I do wish you'd given us a little more warning Andrea. The room really isn't set up for you anymore."

"Mom, I had to get out of there," Andrea said. "It was killing me. Really. I'll sleep on the floor if I have to. I'll share the closet with ski poles and tennis rackets and inflatable rafts if I have to. But I had to come home. I had to be with people who love me for who I am. You understand, don't you, Mom? Tell me you understand."

"I do, honey," Mom said, and she got up and gave Andrea a hug. I thought I could see both of them wipe tears away.

"I can't practice in the living room," Paul said. "This is crazy."

"Fine," Andrea said. "Then let's swap bedrooms. I'll take yours and you can take mine. Then you can practice in your room with no problems."

"I'm not going to give up my bedroom," Paul said. "Not when I just got it to myself. I've had to share that room since I was born, and now I finally have it the way I want it, without all of Mark's junk all over the place, and you want me to give it up?"

"Men," Andrea said with a shrug. "All right, Paul, if it'll make you happy, I'll sleep on the streets. I'm sure I can find some unlocked cars around somewhere that I can crawl into for a few hours' sleep."

"You could move in with Cathy," Paul said. "If I've had to share a room, I don't see why she can get away with not sharing."

"Paul!" I screeched. "I can't share with Andrea."

"Why not?" he asked. "I think it's a fine solution."

"Andrea is a grown-up," I said. "She's twice as old as I am. Besides, my bedroom is only big enough for one bed."

"If you took your desk out there'd be room for two," he said. "Or if you just threw out some of those dumb teddy bears you keep hanging on to."

"You can be so mean, Paul!" I cried.

"Will everybody calm down for a minute, please," Dad said. "I'm starting to get very angry at everybody, and I don't like it. We should be happy that Andrea has come to stay for a while. We shouldn't be ready to tear each other to shreds over this."

"He started it," I said.

"I did not," Paul said. "Andrea did."

"I did," Andrea said. "Paul's absolutely right. I'll go right now and find an unlocked car."

"You'll stay right here," Mom said. "In your old room. You and Paul can work out some sort of schedule so he can continue to practice in there. And we'll move the TV set out into the living room for the duration of Andrea's stay."

"Thanks, Mom," Andrea said. "I used to brag about you too, to my friends."

"That's very nice, dear," Mom said.

"Andrea, honey, what do you plan to do for the next six months besides repair your psychic energies?" Dad asked. "I know that's going to be a time-consuming activity, but do you have any other plans?"

"I don't intend to sit around eating and watching TV if that's what you mean, Dad," Andrea said.

"That's exactly what I mean," he replied.

"I plan to exercise every single day," she said. "Maybe Paul can teach me some of his exercises. I used to dance too, remember, although I was never very good at it. And I'd like to take up the violin again. I only gave it up because Harvey made me."

"Exercises and the violin," Dad said, nodding thoughtfully. "That sounds like a well-balanced program."

"And I'm going to read," Andrea said.

"Books by non-Russians. Maybe even some best-sellers so I can get a fix on what American popular culture is really about. Mom, can you get me the top best-sellers from the library tomorrow?"

"Most of them are on the reserve list," Mom said. "And even if I am a librarian, I can't automatically get them. But I can reserve them if you're willing to wait."

"If I have to wait too long, they won't be best-sellers anymore," Andrea said. "Oh, well. Maybe I'll read some paperbacks instead. I also want to get to know your business better, Dad. I am your firstborn after all, and Mark is planning on physical therapy as a career, and Paul's going to be a soloist for the New York City Ballet, and as far as I know Cathy's never shown any interest in genetic engineering. Have you, pumpkin?"

I shook my head. I know Dad loves his pharmaceutical company, but it gives me the willies just to think about genetic engineering.

"Genetic engineering is a very specialized field," Dad said. "I'd love to have you get involved with it, but you'll need at least a Ph.D. in biology or chem to get even an entry-level job."

"I know I'm not qualified, Dad," Andrea said. "And to be perfectly honest I have no interest in science. That was always Harvey's interest. But there's got to be a lot of business management that doesn't require a science background. After all, you don't go to the office every day and play with a test tube. You push numbers around."

"I run the company," Dad said a little stiffly. "That's not quite the same as pushing numbers."

"All I want to do is check it out," Andrea said. "I'll pretend to be a little mouse sitting in the corner; you won't even know I'm there."

"Don't pretend to be a mouse, dear," Mom said. "They do their experiments on mice."

"Good point," Andrea said. "I'll pretend to be an M.B.A. instead."

"I do hope you intend to help around the house, Andrea," Dad said. "In addition to running my company, that is."

"Absolutely, Dad," Andrea said. "I can't tell you how happy I am you asked me that. I intend to cook supper every single night for this family. Unless I start dating again, and I'm out all the time. But on every night that I don't have a date, I'll be in the kitchen cooking my heart out."

"We don't want to eat your heart, Andrea," Paul said.

"I think dance is limiting your brain, Paul," Andrea said. "Do you ever do anything besides pirouettes?"

"Children, please," Mom said. "Andrea, I thought you hated cooking."

"That was all Harvey's doing," Andrea said. "Do you know, he had me completely convinced that cooking was drudge work just like housecleaning. Now I know you feel that way about housecleaning, Mom, and you're absolutely right; there's nothing more demeaning than dusting except maybe defrosting the refrigerator, which I wouldn't do on a dare. But cooking is as creative as painting, as writing, even as dance, my darling brother. Cooking is an art, one men have been trying to steal from women. But this woman intends to grab it back from male clutches."

"You have my blessings," Dad said. "I hate cooking."

"You'll never have to cook again," Andrea said. "Tomorrow I'll go to the supermarket and buy all kinds of wonderful ingredients and cook this family a meal the likes of which you've never tasted before."

"That's what we're afraid of," Paul said.

It isn't often that I agree with Paul about anything. But this time he had a point. Having Andrea back was going to be like nothing I'd ever had to live with before, and even though I was glad to have her back, I was more than a little afraid of what it was going to mean.

"What little worriers you are," Andrea said, staring straight at me. "I'm back in the loving bosom of my family, and from now on everything is going to be much, much better."

I sure hoped she knew what she was talking about.

Chapter 5

It seemed like every day at lunch Jessica would suggest we go to Comptons for ice-cream cones after school, and every day of course we said yes. So every day she and Amy and Michelle and Libby and I would get our jackets and our books, and walk the couple of blocks to Comptons, and stand on line forever until we got our cones.

Comptons was a nice place, except for Mrs. Compton. There used to be a Mr. Compton, but he disappeared before Andrea went to junior high. She said she'd heard that Mrs. Compton had poisoned him with her rocky road, but probably he just moved out because of his wife's personality. I know I would have. But the place had an old player piano, which Mrs. Compton wouldn't let us use, and some real old pinball machines that she wouldn't even let us stand near, and great ice cream. It was a real ice-cream parlor, with little round tables, and red and white chairs, but she didn't like us to sit at the tables, and if too many of the kids tried to, she'd shoo us all out of there.

"I don't need your business!" she would scream at us. "Go away and bother somebody else."

Frankly I'm surprised nobody poisoned her rocky road, but instead kids at the junior high kept going there year after year. The ice cream really was terrific. Mrs. Compton made only six flavors a day, but four of them would be different from one day to the next (she always had plain old chocolate and vanilla in case you didn't want anything more exciting), and she used really good ingredients. "No chemicals," she would announce as she gave us our cones. "Chemicals rot your minds and teeth."

"Sugar rots your teeth," my mother said when I told her what Mrs. Compton had said. "Including Mrs. Compton's."

But still I liked the idea that there were no chemicals in the ice cream. Andrea swore there were no chemicals in the stuff she was making for us every night, but her food was so weird, chemicals might have improved it. That was a major reason why I was so happy to go to Comptons every day. I never knew from one night to the next if I'd be able to eat what Andrea had prepared. At least I knew I'd had a chemical-free ice-cream cone for nourishment, no matter what showed up on my dinner plate.

As I stared at the different flavors, trying to decide what to order, I remembered the supper we'd had the night before. "It's nouvelle cuisine," Andrea explained to us as she served her latest creation. "Very chic. Just the right way to eat for this decade, don't you think?"

"I like it," Paul said, wolfing down what was on his plate. The portions were tiny, which was a help when the food was inedible, but very discouraging when the food was pretty good. And you never knew which it was going to be. "I'd like some more, please."

"There isn't any more," Andrea declared. "The whole idea behind nouvelle cuisine is to keep the meals light."

"There's light and there's invisible," Dad said. "Your mother and I have both put in hard days at our jobs, Andrea. We'd like to be greeted with something a little more filling than three string beans and an artichoke."

"Oh, Dad, what a tease you can be," Andrea said. "You know perfectly well the doctor's been after you for years to take off ten pounds. On the old style of French cooking that would be impossible. But with nouvelle cuisine you'll eat magnificent meals and never realize you're dieting."

"I think I'll realize it," Dad said. "Marge, do we have any bread in the house? I think I'll make myself a grilled cheese sandwich."

"We're all out," Andrea replied. "I threw it out this morning. Terrible bread, full of chemicals. Did you ever read the list of ingredients? It turns your stomach."

"At least it fills my stomach," Dad grumbled. He and Paul fought over the last string bean, and I decided to move on to double scoops at Comptons from then on.

"You, dummy," I heard Mrs. Compton shout. It took a gentle prod from Libby to make me realize Mrs. Compton was shouting at me. "What flavor do you want, or are you too stupid to know?"

"Van . . . vanilla," I stammered. I blushed from the time I ordered it until I finally got away from the counter with my cone.

"She can be so mean," Libby whispered to me as we joined the other girls at one of the tables. I just nodded and hoped Jessica hadn't seen what had happened. My friendship with Jessica hadn't been getting anywhere as it was, and I didn't need a setback. It wasn't like Jessica was rude to me. She was very polite, but I wanted our friendship to be more than her being polite to me. I wanted her to call me at night and giggle with me on the phone for hours, the way Francie and Mary Kay and I used to do. So that afternoon, to make myself feel better, I gave her my phone number, in case she decided to call.

"Thank you, Cathy," Jessica said, as she examined the piece of paper I'd handed her. "But if this is your phone number, you already gave it to me."

"I did?" I squeaked. I'd developed an awful tendency to squeak around Jessica. I never squeaked anywhere else.

"Last week," she said, and smiled kindly at me. "Thank you, but I really don't need two copies." She handed back the neatly folded piece of paper.

"I'll take it, Cathy," Libby said. "I have to look up your number in the phone book whenever I want to call you."

"Sure, take it," I said, glad someone wanted it. I'd been sure Jessica didn't have my number and that was why she never called. Now I had to figure out a different excuse why she didn't call, and I knew that would be tough.

"Doesn't Comptons make the best fudge

ripple?" Jessica said as Libby put my phone number in her looseleaf. I had gone to Comptons with Jessica and Amy and Michelle and Libby nine times that month, and Mrs. Compton had shouted at me three times. And Jessica had never called me once.

"The ice cream here is the best I've ever eaten," Libby said. "My father says the same thing too. He takes Mom and me here sometimes after we've gone to the movies."

"Does your brother Paul ever come here?" Michelle asked me. "You know, the cute brother you won't let us meet."

"You can meet him," I said, taking a lick of the vanilla. "He's just busy a lot of the time."

"What's he busy with?" Michelle asked. "Maybe I could become busy with it too."

"Just stuff," I said. I still hadn't told them about Paul's dancing. I was pretty sure it would be okay, but I didn't want to take any chances until Jessica started phoning me.

"You are so selfish," Michelle said. "Hogging a big brother to yourself like that, instead of letting us all share him."

"Honestly, Michelle," Amy said. "It isn't like Cathy has any fun with Paul. They just live in the same house, that's all."

"If I had a big brother, you can be sure

I'd let you all meet him," Michelle said. "I'd love to have any one of you be my sister-in-law someday."

We all giggled. I imagined Michelle married to Paul and giggled even harder.

"I'd invite everybody to supper at my house so you could meet Paul," I said, "except my sister is doing the cooking now, and she doesn't like to cook big meals."

"I'll have to have everybody over at my house someday," Jessica said. "Of course Libby practically grew up there, and Amy and Michelle have been there lots of times, so it won't be too exciting for them."

"I love going to your house," Amy said really fast. "It's always so clean."

"My mother insists on that," Jessica said. "She says no person can ever be thought of as being truly personally clean unless the house he or she lives in is spotless as well."

I tried to picture my mother saying anything like that and nearly choked. She did say once, "The only clean house is a dead house," but this didn't seem the time to mention it.

"You, over there!" Mrs. Compton shouted to a boy who was standing six inches away from the player piano. "Get out of here at once!"

"What did I do?" the boy asked.

"Get out!" she shrieked. "Before I call the police, get out!"

So the boy left. I knew exactly how he felt.

"She drives me crazy," I said softly to the other girls as we watched the boy leave. "We ought to stop eating here or something."

"She can be mean," Jessica said. "But maybe she's mean because she's unhappy."

"Sure she's unhappy," I said. "Anyone that mean is bound to be unhappy."

"Maybe she was afraid he was going to damage the piano," Michelle said. "Sometimes I don't think you have too much respect for personal property, Cathy."

"What?" I asked.

"Sometimes your clothes are really sloppy," Michelle said. "Amy and Jessica and I discussed it. Your hems are always coming down, and once your blouse was missing a button."

I couldn't believe this afternoon. First Mrs. Compton, and then Jessica already having my phone number, and now Michelle. "No one in my family sews," I said, trying to keep my voice from quavering. "We do lots of things with safety pins. But everything is clean, honest."

"I'm sure it is," Jessica said. "Michelle shouldn't have even mentioned it. It just came up one day, and we all thought you'd look so much better if you were just a little bit neater. That's all."

No wonder Jessica never called me. It was my hems. "Maybe Andrea sews," I said. "She never used to, but she never used to cook, either."

"My mother sews," Michelle said. "She even does needlepoint. And she cooks, too. Real food."

"Michelle!" Jessica said, but then she smiled. "How about all of you coming over to my house now? We could all do our homework together."

"Okay," Michelle grumbled.

"I don't think I can," I said, feeling like my heart was going to break on the spot. "Tonight's my mom's late night at the library, and Dad has a meeting and they have the cars, so there's no way I could get home. Unless maybe your mother could give me a lift."

"My mother doesn't give lifts," Jessica answered. "She says as soon as a woman starts giving people lifts, she becomes a chauffeur and it simply never ends."

I knew I was going to have to meet Jessica's mother someday. Right then, though, I wasn't sure if I really wanted to.

"My mother gives lifts all the time," Libby said, as we started to walk out of

Comptons. "But she's busy this afternoon, so I don't think we should go to my place."

"Some other time then," Jessica said. "Goodbye, Cathy. See you tomorrow."

"Right, Jessica," I said. "Bye, everybody."

Libby and I started walking one way, and Amy and Michelle followed Jessica the other way. I wanted to join Jessica so much it hurt, but she lived a couple of miles away from me and there was no way to get home.

"Cheer up, Cathy," Libby said. "It's not the end of the world not going to Jessica's house."

"I know," I said. "I'm probably not neat enough to get in anyway."

Libby giggled. "Jessica does like to carry on about neatness," she said. "She kind of has to. Her parents get really angry if their house is untidy. I was there once when Jessica had left her doll in the living room and her father had a fit."

"My house is really sloppy," I said. "Want to come over and see for yourself?"

"I'd love to," Libby said. "Are you sure it's okay?"

"Oh, yeah," I said. "Nobody's home except maybe Andrea, and she stays in her room a lot. She ponders in there about her future."

"I can't wait to meet her," Libby said. "She sounds crazy but nice."

"I guess she is," I said. "It's been weird having her home. I never really knew her, you know, and now she's cooking supper and telling me about the way the world is, and all kinds of junk."

"I'd like an older sister like that," Libby said. "It gets kind of lonely being an only child."

"Jessica's an only child too," I said. "Do you think she gets lonely?"

"Probably," Libby said.

"I'm never lonely," I said. "Sometimes I'd like to be though."

Libby laughed. "My mother always says you want what you can't have." Then she laughed even harder. "I sound like Jessica now, saying what my mother always says."

"I'd like to sound like Jessica," I admitted. "I love the way she talks. Like a grown-up almost."

"Oh, I can talk like that too," Libby said. "When you're an only child it's real easy to talk like a grown-up. I just think it sounds dumb, so I don't."

"Do you really think Jessica sounds dumb?" I asked.

"No, I guess not," Libby said with a sigh. "No dumber than the rest of us."

We walked silently together for almost two blocks, and then Libby turned to me. "Is your house really a mess?" she asked.

"The pits," I said. "A regular junk heap."

"It sounds wonderful," Libby said. "I can hardly wait."

Chapter 6

"Are you free Saturday night?" Libby asked me on the first Wednesday in October.

"Of course I am," I replied. We were in the cafeteria, and I kept looking for Jessica and the others. The five of us had lunch every day now, so Libby knew what I was searching for.

"How about coming over to my house for a sleepover," she suggested. " I just got the new Hot Tomato album, and it's really good."

"That sounds great," I said. "Can I come for supper?"

"Of course," Libby said. "Saturday night Dad cooks, and he makes a big pot of spaghetti and meat sauce. There's enough for twenty."

"That sounds so great," I said. "Andrea is preparing an extra-special meal for

Saturday, so I'd really like to eat someplace else."

Libby laughed. "How long is Andrea going to keep cooking?" she asked.

"Until she's tried every single recipe in that new book she got," I said glumly. "And there are five hundred recipes in it. We're only on number twenty-one, so it's going to be years."

"Well, if you don't mind good old-fashioned spaghetti and meat sauce, things'll be fine," Libby said.

"What about spaghetti?" Amy asked, plopping her tray next to mine. "Spaghetti is my absolute favorite."

"Even more than pizza?" Libby asked.

"Even more than ice cream," Amy replied. "Maybe not as much as chocolate though. Chocolate fudge first, and then spaghetti."

"That's what Libby's dad is cooking on Saturday," I explained.

"I haven't had spaghetti in ages," Amy said. "My mother is on this diet, and she refuses to cook anything with starch in it. I swear all we eat are carrots and string beans."

"You have spaghetti in school," Libby pointed out. "They serve it a lot."

"That's not real spaghetti," Amy said.

"Here, Michelle." She waved and Michelle saw us and came over. "Doesn't spaghetti and meat sauce sound just wonderful?" she asked, as Michelle sat down next to her.

"Where is it?" Michelle asked.

"At Libby's, Saturday night," Amy said. "Do you think there'd be enough for me too, Lib?"

"I guess so," Libby said. "Dad makes a ton of it."

"I always knew I'd like your father," Amy said. "I can't believe I'll actually get to eat real food."

"Where's Jessica?" I asked.

"She's talking to Mr. Flynn," Michelle said, taking a big swallow of milk. "He gave her an 88 on her test, and she thinks she should have gotten a 90. So she's talking to him about it."

"It was a hard test," I said. I'd gotten a 92, but I'd guessed right on a couple of things I really didn't know. So I deserved an 88 just as much as Jessica did.

"Jessica's parents really like her to get good grades," Libby said. "That's always been a big deal for them."

"I'll say," Michelle replied. "Last year one of her teachers gave her an 82 on her report card, and her father went to the teacher and argued about it for half an hour. Jessica still ended up with the 82, and her parents took away her weekend privileges for a whole month."

"Wow," I said. "My parents would be thrilled if I got 82s on my report card."

"Don't be silly, Cathy," Libby said. "I've seen your grades. You're really smart."

"I'm not that smart," I said. "Besides my brother Mark used to help me study. Only now he's in college, and I'll probably flunk everything."

"There's Jessica now," Amy said. "We're over here!" she called out. Jessica heard her and came over.

"Did you get the two extra points?" Michelle asked as Jessica sat down next to Libby. She was sitting across from me and I could see she was upset.

"He said I shouldn't care so much," Jessica said. "That grades shouldn't be so important. I'm only eleven, he said. I have plenty of time to worry about my grades."

"That's terrible," Amy said.

"Teachers can be so dumb sometimes," I said. "I can't believe how thoughtless Mr. Flynn is."

"My father is going to be furious," Jessica said. "I told him I'd get at least a 90 on the test. Now I don't know what to do."

"Can't you lie?" Michelle asked. "I'm

always telling my parents I did better on tests than I really did. They never ask to see them and by the time I get my report card, they've forgotten what I told them anyway."

"Dad asks to see them," Jessica said. "He likes to go over tests with me, so we can work out my mistakes together. He says kids don't learn from their mistakes enough. After we go over the mistakes, he always makes up new questions and tests me on them to make sure I've learned what I got wrong before."

If I had ever wondered why Jessica was perfect, now I had the answer. Both her parents worked on it day and night with her. If my parents had devoted half that much time to me, I'd end up president of the United States by high school.

"Don't be too upset," Amy said. "Libby's invited us all over to her house for Saturday night spaghetti. Doesn't that sound great?"

"Oh, yeah," Jessica said, and she gave Libby a half-smile. "Her father makes great spaghetti. I've had it lots of times."

"After the spaghetti, we're having a sleepover," I added. "It should be a great night, Jessica. Say you'll come."

"If my dad will let me," she said. "Sometimes he gets kind of mad if my grades aren't good enough."

"But you got an 88," I said. "It isn't like you flunked or anything."

"I'm sure it'll be okay," she said. "How did you do on the test, Cathy?"

"I got an 86," I said real fast. I didn't like lying, but Jessica was so upset I didn't want her to feel worse. "It was a really tough test."

"I'll tell Dad you said that," Jessica said.

"So it's set," I declared. "We're all going to have spaghetti and a sleepover at Libby's Saturday night." I thought I saw Libby give me a funny look, but when she didn't say anything I figured I'd made it up.

"That sounds great," Michelle said. "But I don't suppose we could invite any boys over?"

"Michelle!" Amy screeched, and soon we were all laughing and acting perfectly normal again.

Libby and I walked home from school that day without stopping at Comptons. Jessica had a piano lesson, so there didn't seem any point in going there. "Why did you mention the sleepover?" Libby asked me when we'd gotten two blocks away from the school.

"What do you mean?" I asked.

"I hadn't planned on inviting everybody," Libby said. "I asked my mother if you could stay over and she said that was fine, but now I have to ask her if Amy and Michelle and Jessica can stay too."

"She won't mind, will she?" I asked. "I thought you said your mother likes it when your friends come over."

"Of course she does," Libby said. "But you shouldn't have invited everybody like that, without asking me first."

"You'd invited them all over for spaghetti," I said. "I just assumed it was okay."

"Okay," Libby said. "I suppose it was an accident."

"Look, if it'll make things better I won't come," I said. "Then it'll just be the four of you."

"Don't be silly," Libby said sharply. "You're the one who's invited. Of course you can come."

"It'll be fun," I said. "And Jessica looked so unhappy about her grade, I thought we should do something to cheer her up."

"You really got an 86?" Libby asked me.

"What?" I said, and for a moment I didn't know what she was talking about. "Oh, on the English test? Sure. What did you get?"

"I got a 90," Libby said. "But I saw the test papers when they were being handed back, and I could have sworn I saw you got a 90 something."

"You got a 90?" I asked. "That's great. Congratulations."

"I studied hard," Libby said.

"I guess I should have too," I said, wishing I could end the dumb lie. "I think it was mean of Mr. Flynn not to raise Jessica's grade."

"Jessica gets away with murder," Libby said. "If all she deserved was an 88, then why should Mr. Flynn raise her grade?"

I shrugged my shoulders.

"Sometimes she makes me so mad," Libby said. "You weren't upset about your grade after all, and you didn't do as well as she did. You didn't go crying to Mr. Flynn and begging him to give you some more points you didn't deserve. Jessica expects the whole world to do exactly what she wants it to do."

"It wasn't that important to me," I said. "That's all. I don't have a father who goes over my mistakes with me. My dad just expects me to make them. He says people aren't interesting unless they make mistakes every now and again."

"It isn't just her father," Libby said. "You don't know Jessica as well as I do, Cathy. She really expects the world to revolve around her. It makes me sick sometimes to see the way Amy and Michelle fetch and carry for her."

"I thought you liked Jessica," I said. "I thought you were friends."

"Sure she's my friend," Libby replied. "She just makes me sick sometimes."

I bit my lower lip. If Libby wasn't going to stay friends with Jessica I didn't know what I'd do. Libby and I walked home from school together every single day, and she'd gotten to expect us to have lunch together too. She even called me on the phone at night sometimes. Jessica still didn't do that, and I really wasn't sure if I stopped having lunch with her she'd even notice. Libby just had to stay friends with Jessica, until Jessica and I became best friends.

"I think maybe you're mad at me," I said. "For inviting everybody to the sleep-over and you really aren't mad at Jessica at all."

"I guess I am mad at you too," Libby said.

"I'm sorry," I said. "I'm always saying stuff I shouldn't say. I'll tell you what."

"What?" Libby asked, and I could see she was thinking about smiling.

"How about if I come over to your house right now with you and I tell your mother just what happened, and how it was my fault everybody got invited," I said. "That way she won't be mad at you because she'll see it was my fault. And if she doesn't want us all over, I'll see if my mom would mind and we could all have supper at your house and sleep over at mine. How's that?"

"Is there room for all of us at your house?" Libby asked.

"No," I said. "But we can squeeze in somewhere."

"If you're really willing to talk to my mother," Libby said. "Sure, come on over."

So instead of walking back to my house, I went on with Libby. I didn't know what I was going to say to her mother when I actually saw her, but at least Libby wasn't mad at Jessica anymore, and that was the important thing.

I'd never been to Libby's house before, or met either of her parents, so I felt funny about it. But her house turned out to look perfectly normal. It was more modern than my house and I was sure it had more closets even before Libby unlocked the front door and I could see how neat it was.

I liked the little bit of clutter Libby had promised me. There were a couple of magazines on the coffee table, and an opened book on an end table. That was the clutter, and I thought it looked great. No ballet shoes, no paring knives, no opened briefcases with papers scattered all over the sofa. No piles of library books, and for that matter, no dolls or teddy bears. And the curtains didn't look like they were being held together with thumbtacks, the way they are in my house. If that was slightly cluttered, I could hardly wait to see what Jessica's spotless house looked like.

"Mom," Libby called out, "I'm home."

"That's nice," her mother called back. "I'm in the kitchen."

I tried to imagine what it must be like to come home from school and have my mother in the kitchen. But my mother had been working for too many years for me even to be able to imagine.

"Come on," Libby said, and she half pushed me through a hallway and into the kitchen. Her kitchen was a lot more modern than ours, and the food her mother was cooking smelled a lot better than anything Andrea had cooked for over two weeks now. "Mom, this is Cathy," Libby said. "She came home with me."

"Great," Libby's mother said, and she wiped her hands on her apron before shaking mine. I loved it. My mother's idea of an apron is to tuck a dish towel under her belt. "Hi, Cathy. Libby's told me so much about you."

"Hi," I said shyly. "I'm just here to say it's all my fault."

Libby's mother looked at me and laughed. "Would you like something to eat or drink?" she asked. "I have some date nut bars I baked yesterday."

"They're really good," Libby said. "And you'd better eat something if you're going to have supper at home tonight."

"I'd love one," I said.

"And some milk?" her mother asked, and I nodded. Libby sat down at the kitchen table, and I took the chair next to hers. Her mother went to the refrigerator and took out the milk. She brought it and the date nut bars to the table and we all took one and a glass of milk. "What's your fault, Cathy?"

"I have a big mouth," I said, trying to remember not to talk while I chewed. It wasn't easy, since the date nut bars were pretty chewy. "You see, Libby invited me over for supper Saturday night and to sleep over and I said yes."

"Good," her mother said. "I was hoping you would."

"But then somehow everybody got invited for supper," I continued. "I don't think I did that, but maybe that was my fault too."

"No," Libby said. "That wasn't your fault. Is it okay, Mom, if Jessica, Amy, and Michelle have supper here too?"

"No problem," her mother said. "You know how your father loves to cook that meat sauce. He'll just make lots extra. We'll have garlic bread too. How does that sound?"

"It sounds perfect," I said. "My sister Andrea's been cooking such terrible meals, you can't imagine how good garlic bread sounds."

"Fine," her mother said. "Then that's settled."

"No, it isn't," I said, gulping down the last of the date nut bar so I could talk right away. "You see that's when it's all my fault."

"Oh," Libby's mother said. "I'm afraid you're going to have to explain all this to me."

"I invited everybody else to sleep over," I said. "It just kind of happened, but now Amy and Michelle and Jessica expect to stay over here Saturday night, only Libby said you hadn't said they could. You hadn't said they couldn't either, though, but if you do, I mean if you don't want us all, then everybody can stay at my house even though it'll be kind of crowded because of my sister Andrea. She takes up a lot of room. But really, it'll be okay."

"What's the problem?" Libby's mother asked. "Libby's had four girls over for sleepovers before, and there's been plenty of space."

"It's really okay, Mom?" Libby asked.

"It sure is," her mother said. "Cathy, have another date nut bar. It sounds like they're starving you at home."

"Just about," I said, feeling a lot cheerier. Libby's mother was so nice, it was hard to believe I'd thought there might be a problem. "I'd love another date nut bar, thank you very much."

Chapter 7

Libby and I walked home together from Comptons the next afternoon. We mostly talked about the sleepover while we were there, but Libby hadn't seemed mad at me, which was kind of a relief. She'd flinched once when Michelle mentioned inviting boys over too, but that had been about it, and Jessica had told Michelle that of course we couldn't do that, so Libby didn't have to. On the whole, I figured I'd gotten off pretty easy.

We reached the corner of my street before Libby's. Usually we said goodbye there, and Libby kept on walking to her house alone. But that afternoon I decided to ask Libby if she wanted to come over.

"I'd love to," Libby said, practically before I got the words out. So we walked the extra half-block together.

"Andrea, I'm home!" I called as soon as I came in.

"Glad to hear it," Andrea replied, walking into the living room. She came from the direction of the kitchen, which could only mean she'd been hard at work on one of her dinners. I sighed at the thought.

"Andrea, this is Libby," I said. Andrea had been in her room last time, so they hadn't met. "This is my sister Andrea," I told Libby. "The one who cooks."

"I do other things," Andrea said, and extended her hand for Libby to shake. Which Libby did, with a smile on her face. I was impressed with both of them. "It's nice to meet you, Libby. Cathy's mentioned you a lot lately. You and Jessica."

"We used to be friends a long time ago," Libby said. "And now we're friends again."

"I like that," Andrea said. "Come on into the kitchen. I'm hard at work on dinner. A culinary masterpiece, if I do say so myself."

"Yeah, let's go into the kitchen," I said, glancing uneasily around the living room. One good thing about Andrea taking over the kitchen was that it was relatively neat. At least compared to the rest of the house.

If Libby noticed how messy everything

was, she didn't say anything. She just followed Andrea into the kitchen.

"Why don't you stay for supper, Libby?" Andrea asked. "There's plenty of food if you want."

"There's never plenty of food," I said. "How can there possibly be enough for Libby too?"

"Because Paul called ten minutes ago to say he was going to have supper at Robby's," Andrea said. "So there's an extra portion of everything available if Libby is interested."

"I'd love it," Libby said. "Let me call my mom and make sure it's okay with her."

"There's a phone right here," Andrea said, pointing to the one on the wall. Libby picked up the receiver and dialed home before I even had a chance to decide whether I wanted her for supper or not.

It was probably okay, I decided, especially since Paul wasn't going to be there. The house was horrible, with piles piled on top of piles, but Libby hadn't seemed to mind the last time. And it wasn't like she was Jessica. If I ever got Jessica to come over, things were going to be absolutely perfect. With Libby, things could be more comfortable.

It was a good thing I'd decided that, since Libby's mother said it was fine for

Libby to stay for supper. Andrea immediately put us to work scrubbing baby potatoes.

"All the vitamins are in the skin," Andrea informed us. "Without the skin, there's practically no point eating the things."

"That's what my father says," Libby replied. "He's a doctor, and he's very interested in nutrition."

"I'll have to invite him for dinner someday," Andrea said. "We can discuss nutrition and diet in contemporary America."

"I'm sure he'd like that," Libby answered, but I could tell from the giggle in her eyes that she wasn't sure at all.

Right then the phone rang. I jumped up, startled by the sound, and since I was already in the air, I answered the phone. "Hello?"

"I want to talk to Andrea," the voice on the other end declared.

It took me a moment to recognize the voice, and then I did. "Harvey?" I squeaked. "Is that you, Harvey?"

"Yeah, it is," Harvey said. "Cathy, is Andrea there?"

"I guess so," I said. But before I had a chance to ask Andrea if she wanted to talk to him, she'd already picked up the phone.

"I can't talk now, Harvey," Andrea said. "Besides, don't you know to wait until after five o'clock when the rates go down?"

I guess Harvey said something then because Andrea was silent for a moment before she spoke again. "Yes, I got the cookbook," she said. "Thank you, Harvey, that was really very nice of you. Not adequate perhaps for all the pain and desolation you've made me endure, but nice. A good shot, Harvey. Try to weasel your way back into my affections by pretending to be interested in what I care about. I know your tricks, Harvey. You can't fool me anymore."

She was silent for another few seconds, and then she said, "Look, Harvey, I have to hang up now. There are some very important people in the kitchen here with me, and I want to devote my total attention to them. The way you never did with me, Harvey. Yes, Harvey. Goodbye, Harvey. And if you must call me again, call when the rates are lower." She hung up the phone with a flourish, and then stared at it for a moment.

"Harvey sent you a cookbook?" I asked.

"Where do you think I've been getting all these fabulous recipes?" Andrea said. "He says he'll do anything to win me back, but of course he's lying."

"How do you know he's lying?" Libby asked.

"A woman knows these things," Andrea declared grandly. "Besides, even if he isn't lying, I'm still not interested."

"But how did he know you were cooking?" I asked. "You didn't cook when you lived in Boston."

"This isn't the first time he's called," Andrea said. "And always before five o'clock. Naturally I've kept the conversations as brief as possible, but he's wormed things out of me anyway."

"That creep Harvey always was a worm," I said, as much to Libby as to Andrea.

"I suppose," Andrea said. "I just hope all these negative vibrations won't affect dinner."

"I'm sure they won't," Libby said. "It takes a lot to kill good cooking."

"Good point," Andrea said. "I like you Libby. You understand the important things."

I felt a little left out, not understanding the important things. But I'd eaten nothing but Andrea's cooking lately, and I didn't think it would take very many negative vibrations to kill the last three weeks of dinners we'd had.

"Oh, Cathy," Andrea said, trying to sound casual. "You don't have to mention to Mom and Dad that Harvey called. It can be our little secret."

"Why don't you want them to know?" I asked.

"You know Dad," Andrea said. "He turns purple just at the mention of Harvey. This dinner's been exposed to enough bad vibrations. Why risk things further?"

"Okay then," I said. "For the sake of dinner."

Andrea smiled at me. "You are a remarkable young woman, Cathy," she declared. "You have an extraordinary understanding of the truly important things."

After that I felt better, and even offered to set the table. So when Mom came in, what she saw first was my being industrious, and then she noticed Libby.

"Libby's staying for supper, okay, Mom?" I said "It's okay with her mother. She already called and asked. And there's going to be enough food, because Paul is having supper at Robby's."

"It's fine with me," Mom said. "We don't exactly have more than enough to go around these days, Libby, but what there is is certainly interesting."

"I can always eat something when I get home," Libby said. "Mom always has stuff in the refrigerator."

"Maybe I'll go over with you," Mom said and then she laughed. "I shouldn't make so much fun of Andrea's cooking," she said. "She's a much better cook than I ever dreamed of being."

"I miss your cooking anyway, Mom," I told her.

"I miss it sometimes too," Mom admitted. "Oh, well, your father is losing weight, and that's something."

"Dinner is cooking," Andrea announced, walking into the dining room. "And the table is set, thank you, Cathy, so why don't we go into the living room for a while?"

So we all did. Mom kicked off her shoes as soon as she sat down on the couch. With a pang, I remembered how neat Libby's living room had been.

"We're all slobs around here," Mom said, as though she were reading my thoughts. "I hope that doesn't bother you, Libby."

"No, of course not," Libby said.

"Good," Mom said. "Because, to be perfectly honest, there isn't much we can do about it now. Cathy's father and I are both basically messy people, so neither one of us is capable of stopping the other one. I think it drives Cathy crazy sometimes."

"I don't mind too much," I said.

"Mind what?" Dad asked, coming in. I hadn't heard him at the front door. "Dinner certainly smells good tonight, Andrea. What is it?"

"Trout poached in white wine sauce," Andrea replied. "Baby potatoes and string beans."

"That sounds great," Libby said. "You have stuff like that every night here?"

"I try," Andrea said. "Of course these barbarians would rather I just made hot dogs. But I'm working on improving their palates."

"My palate is uneducated and starved," Dad said. "I hope there's going to be enough for all of us."

"There should be," Mom said. "Paul is at Robby's, and Libby has graciously agreed to eat his dinner here."

"Thank you, Libby," Dad said, dropping his briefcase to the floor. "It will be nice having an unbiased opinion of Andrea's cooking."

"I'll try to be unbiased," Libby said. "But I helped wash the potatoes."

"Then you just won't be allowed to eat them," Dad said. "That way there'll be another potato for me."

"No way," Libby said. "That potato is mine!"

Everybody laughed. I couldn't believe how easily Libby fit in with my family. Of course I'd felt comfortable with her mother too, but I just figured that was because her mother was so nice, and not quite as crazy as everybody in my family. And not having Paul around was a help. But even so, Libby seemed right at home, joking with everybody, and not saying anything about the shoes and the briefcases.

I thought for one moment about what it would be like having Jessica over for supper unexpectedly like this, but I just couldn't picture Jessica any place that wasn't clean and perfect. The very thought of having Jessica over for supper when things looked the way they did made my stomach turn a lot worse than any of Andrea's cooking ever had.

I promised myself I'd have Jessica over for supper someday, but not until the house, my family, and I were totally prepared.

And then I realized everybody was laughing, and I didn't know why. So I stopped thinking about Jessica and paid attention to what was going on right then then and there.

Chapter 8

Just as I was getting ready to leave for Libby's Saturday evening, the phone rang. I almost didn't bother waiting to find out who it was for, but my feet stopped moving, and I stood still for as long as it took to hear it was Mary Kay for me.

"How're you doing?" I asked her, hoping she'd give me a fast answer. She'd called a couple of times since school started, but we'd only seen each other that one time when it had felt so strange seeing her in her uniform.

"I'm fine," she said. "Look, I had this great idea. Why don't you spend the night at my place? My mom says if you do, and we absolutely swear not to talk for more than fifteen minutes, she'll let us call Chicago and talk to Francie. Wouldn't that be great?"

"Gee, that would be terrific," I said. "But I can't. Not tonight."

"Oh, why?" Mary Kay asked. "Can't you get out of whatever it is?"

"No. I'm going to Libby's for a sleep-over," I said. "Remember Libby?"

"Sure," Mary Kay said. "That's right. You said you were spending a lot of time with her."

She sounded so disappointed that for a second I thought about inviting her to come along too. But I'd been embarrassed enough doing that once, and I wasn't about to take any more chances. "Maybe next weekend," I said. "Maybe you could come over and I could invite Libby and some of the other kids I've gotten friendly with and you could finally meet them."

"That would be nice," Mary Kay said. "Give me a call during the week."

"I'll do that," I promised. "I really have to go now."

"Sure," she said. "Bye, Cathy."

"Bye," I said and hung up. I wished I'd left before the phone rang. But I hadn't, and I wasn't going to feel bad about not seeing Mary Kay so often. Tonight was going to be my first real chance to do something with Jessica and that was the most important thing right now.

I was the first one over at Libby's, but I figured that was because I was the only one in walking distance. Libby seemed happy to see me, and she took me right into the kitchen to meet her father. He was working hard at the stove, stirring and tasting his meat sauce, and after we said hello he had me taste it to see what I thought.

"It's delicious," I said. I hadn't tasted anything that good since Andrea had come back home.

"I think it needs a touch more oregano," he said, and put a touch more in. He was right. The sauce was even better then.

Libby's mother was making the salad, and soon Libby and I joined her, and we all peeled and sliced vegetables together. By the time Jessica, Amy, and Michelle arrived, I felt right at home.

Supper was pretty noisy, with the five of us and Libby's parents all eating and talking and making jokes. I tried really hard not to get spaghetti sauce over anything, and every now and again I'd check on Jessica to see how neatly she ate. She wrapped her spaghetti strands around her fork, and never spilled a drop of sauce. Her mouth didn't even get dirty, although she did touch it occasionally with her napkin.

Amy got sauce all over her blouse, but she said it was okay, so we all just laughed about it. Michelle ate about as neatly as I did, which made me feel better, although I would have loved to have been as neat as Jessica. And Libby kept checking us all out, to make sure we were doing okay. Her father kept telling us to have some more, and her mother fussed over us too, but Libby just watched.

Right in the middle of one of her stares, I remembered that I hadn't told her about Mary Kay's phone call. "Remember Mary Kay?" I asked her. "She called me right before I came over here."

"Who's Mary Kay?" Amy asked, trying to wipe the sauce off her blouse, and just spreading it around.

"She's a friend of mine," I said. "She goes to St. Theresa's now."

"Do they have boys at St. Theresa's?" Michelle asked.

"I think so," I said.

"They're probably babies," Jessica said. "They are in elementary school after all."

"So would we be if they hadn't changed things this year," Libby said.

"But we're not," Jessica said. "Besides I always thought the kids in elementary school were babies."

"The little ones sure are," Amy said.

"I'm glad I don't have to go to school with any kindergarteners."

"Or third graders," Michelle said. "Third graders are the biggest pests."

"Some sixth graders aren't so hot, either," Libby said.

"How about some more garlic bread, girls?" her father asked. "There's practically a whole loaf here."

"I'll have some," I said. I really didn't have an opinion about whether elementary school kids were babies, but if Jessica said so, it was worth thinking about. I just figured I might as well think with my mouth full of garlic bread.

After supper we all had ice-cream cake roll, which is practically my favorite dessert in the world. I thanked Mrs. Katz for having bought it.

"Libby mentioned that you like it," she said. "And I haven't had any in so long, I thought it was a wonderful idea."

I couldn't even remember telling Libby that I liked it, but I guess I must have. It was nice of Libby to remember. I guess everyone liked ice-cream cake roll, because it disappeared almost immediately.

Jessica insisted we do the dishes, so we piled into the kitchen and soon we were scrubbing and drying and flinging soap-suds at each other. I never knew washing dishes could be fun. I guess anything you do with friends is more fun than stuff you do alone.

Libby didn't do the dishes, but she ordered us around, telling us where to put the dishes and silverware and pots and pans. The rest of us took turns washing and drying and flinging soapsuds.

When we finished with the dishes we went to the family room and watched TV for a while with Libby's parents. Then we decided to make popcorn. It turned out Michelle knew all about making popcorn, so we let her do most of it, while we watched. She did know too, and the popcorn was just wonderful. Even in the days when my family ate like normal people, this meal would have been extra special.

We gave some of the popcorn to Libby's parents, and took the rest of it up to Libby's bedroom. Libby's room was absolutely huge, and she'd pushed most of her furniture against the walls, so there was space for cots and sleeping bags. We all took spots to sleep in, and then we changed into our pajamas just to get more comfortable. We certainly didn't plan on going to sleep right then.

Instead we listened to Libby's new record, and we listened to some other records she had. I couldn't get over how good her stereo was. It was practically as nice as the one my whole family shared.

"My parents gave it to me for my birthday last year," she explained.

"My mother suggested it," Jessica said. "When I got one, Libby got one too."

"Our birthdays are a couple of days apart," Libby said. "When we were really little, we used to have birthday parties together."

Libby was so lucky to have known Jessica for so many years. "Those must have been great parties," I said.

"I don't know," Libby said. "They stopped when we were three. I think they did it to save time."

"That's not why my mother did it," Jessica said. "Maybe your mother wanted to save time, but not mine."

"Okay," Libby said. "Just my mother."

"My mother says it's never a waste of time to do something for your child," Jessica said.

I tried to think if my mother had ever said anything like that to me but mostly I remembered her saying "Not now, honey, I don't have the time." She said that almost every day, it seemed to me.

"How about playing some games," Michelle suggested. "Or else maybe inviting some boys to come over."

"We can't have any boys over," Amy said. "We're in our pajamas already."

"Oh, rats," Michelle said. "I guess we'd just have to take them off then."

"Michelle!" Amy screeched.

"No boys," Libby said. "But I do have some games." She went to her closet, and took out a big pile of them. The only problem was most of them were for up to four players. It took us awhile to find one that five could play, and then it turned out Jessica didn't like that game.

"It's so babyish," she said. "I'm surprised you still have it Libby. I threw mine out years ago."

"I like it," Libby said. "When I'm in the right mood."

"I suppose," Jessica said. "I just like older games."

"I like games I can win," I said. "I don't care what age they're for."

"You can win any game," Libby said. "What're you talking about?"

"No, I can't," I said. "I'm the youngest in my family. I never win anything."

"My little brother screams when he doesn't win," Michelle said. "He holds his breath sometimes too, until we let him win. He's really awful."

"I'll have to try that sometime," I said.

"I should be able to hold my breath for quite a while."

So before I knew it, we were all holding our breath to see how long we could and which one of us would hold it the longest. Jessica won, which didn't really surprise me.

"I've been swimming since I was two," she said. "Swimming really helps you hold your breath a long time."

I wondered if her mother had taught her to hold her breath. I could just picture the two of them practicing breath-holding together. That was just the sort of thing my mother wouldn't have the time to do with me.

"I know what we can do," Michelle said. "We can play truth or dare."

"What's that?" Libby asked.

"I never played it, either," I said.

"You mean they didn't play that at South Street?" Amy asked.

"It's really good," Michelle said. "Someone goes first, and she dares someone else to do something. If the girl she dares doesn't do it, or can't, then the first girl gets to ask her anything, and the other girl has to answer it honestly."

"That sounds pretty easy," I said.

"Okay then," Michelle said. "I dare you to hold your breath for thirty seconds."

"Is that all?" I asked. I was sure when we'd all been holding our breaths, I'd held mine for a minute or more. I took a deep breath, and puffed my cheeks out wide and sat absolutely still, trying not to think about breathing. Only about ten seconds later I noticed Libby trying not to giggle and that got me giggling and out came the breath.

"You lose," Michelle said triumphantly. "Now you have to tell me the truth."

"I'm ready," I said, although I really wasn't.

"Why won't you let us meet your brother?" she asked. "Really."

I breathed a sigh of relief. I don't know what I was scared she was going to ask, but I sure was scared of something. "It's because he's weird," I said. "That's all."

"How's he weird?" Michelle asked.

"I don't have to answer that," I said. "You got your one question. Now it's my turn."

"I thought you never played before," Michelle said. "Okay, you go, Cathy. But I'll get you next time, and I'll know just what to ask."

"I'm going to dare Jessica," I said. "I dare you to do a handstand."

"Is that all?" Jessica asked. "That's easy."

"Didn't you know Jessica does gymnastics?" Amy asked me and Jessica bent over, lowered her head to the floor, and did a perfect handstand.

It seemed to me I did know that, but I didn't really believe even Jessica could do a handstand. I should have known it was just another thing she did perfectly.

"Well, I win that round," Jessica said. "Okay, I'm going to challenge Amy. Say 'She sells seashells by the seashore.'"

"That's easy," Amy said. "She sell seashells by the sheashore."

We all laughed at her. "Drat," Amy said. said. "Okay, what do you want to know?"

"Just what did you get on the science test?" Jessica asked. "The one you flunked."

"I got a 62," Amy admitted. "But it wasn't my fault. I had the flu. I was practically dying. I shouldn't have gone to school at all that day, let alone take a test."

"You really got a 62?" Jessica said. "What did your mother say?"

"She said I'd better start passing my tests if I knew what was good for me," Amy replied. "Then she said she never did well in science, either. And then she said maybe I really had been sick that day, and she was sorry she'd sent me to school."

"Wow," Jessica said. "My father would have murdered me."

"Marks aren't that important to my mother," Amy said. "Weight is."

"It's your turn, Amy," Michelle said. "Who are you going to dare?"

"Libby," she said. "I dare Libby to stand on one foot with her eyes closed for a minute."

"What?" Libby said.

"You heard me," Amy said. "On one foot with your eyes closed. I'll bet you can't."

"I'll bet I can't too," Libby said. "But I'll try." She stood up, lifted her left foot off the ground, and closed her eyes. She looked silly too, like a sleeping stork. And sure enough after half a minute or so, she lost her balance.

"My mother taught me that trick," Amy said. "Okay, Libby, you have to answer my question."

"Shoot," Libby said.

"Who do you like best in this room?" Amy asked.

I knew she was going to answer Jessica, the way I would have. But Libby just smiled and said, "I like me the best."

"That's not fair!" Amy said. "I meant after you."

"Then you should have said so," Libby said. "Okay, it's my turn. I'm going to dare Jessica to sing the 'Star-Spangled Banner.' "

"What?" Jessica said. "Oh, Libby, you know that isn't fair."

"Why not?" I asked.

"I'm a terrible singer," Jessica said. "I hate singing in public."

"You can do it," Libby said. "Just pretend you're at Yankee Stadium."

" 'Oh say can you see,' " Jessica piped out. She really did have a bad singing voice. Even I had to admit that.

" 'By the dawn's early light.' Oh, I quit. I hate singing. Ask me anything you want, Libby."

"What do you like least about each of us?" Libby asked.

"Wow," Michelle said. "What a question!"

"About each of you?" Jessica said. "Okay. I don't like how sloppy Amy is. That's easy."

"I wish I weren't so sloppy," Amy said. "I'm working on it."

"And I wish Michelle were a little less boy crazy," Jessica continued. "Just a little. And I think Cathy is immature. And sometimes Libby can be a real snotface."

"What do you mean immature?" I asked.

"Oh, you know," Jessica said. "Sometimes I think you haven't been anywhere or seen anything. You're kind of unsophisticated, you know."

I didn't know. But it sure gave me a lot to think about. Even as we kept on playing, all I could think about was that Jessica thought I was unsophisticated.

I was sure there was a way I could get over that. All I'd have to do was show Jessica my sophisticated side. That shouldn't be too hard. And once that was done, there'd be no reason why Jessica wouldn't like me enough to be best friends.

Chapter 9

"How do you become more sophisticated?" I asked Andrea a couple of days later. We were in the kitchen, where she was preparing veal for dinner. Veal was the most substantial food she'd prepared for us for ages, and I was pretty excited about it, even though I didn't know how she expected to feed five of us on the tiny amount she was making. Still, even two bites of veal was enough to make my mouth water.

"Pass me the garlic press," she said, so I did. "And would you mind chopping those shallots? That would be a big help."

So I chopped shallots.

"Why do you want to be sophisticated?" she asked, about five minutes later. It was amazing what Andrea remembered when you were sure she wasn't paying any attention.

"No reason," I said. "I'm just in junior

high, that's all. I'm not a baby anymore."

"Okay," Andrea said. "I guess that's good enough reason. Just as long as you don't want to be too sophisticated."

"Just a little," I said. "Well, as much as I can get away with."

"You're already a lot more sophisticated than I was when I was your age," Andrea said, pouring white wine into a measuring cup. "I was such a baby when I was eleven. And look at you. You're going to be eating veal cooked in wine sauce on a Monday night."

"I want the kind of sophisticated that shows," I said.

"Food is a major part of being sophisticated," Andrea said. "You are what you eat, after all. And where you eat counts too, and how. You probably have the most sophisticated diet of any eleven-year-old in this town."

"What else can I do?" I asked.

"You can wear high heels," Andrea said. "And designer dresses. And change your name to something sophisticated. Margo, maybe, or Muffy."

"How about just plain Catherine," I said. "Is that a sophisticated name?"

"Very," Andrea said. "Much more sophisticated than Andrea. But I don't think you'll get everybody to call you that. It takes too long."

"Fooey," I said, and bit into a carrot that was just laying around.

"Sophisticated people don't say fooey," Andrea said, taking a carrot for herself. "I have never once met a sophisticated person who said fooey."

"What do they say then?" I asked. I was perfectly willing to give up saying fooey if it meant Jessica would be my best friend.

"They say things Mom and Dad would kill you if you said," Andrea replied. "I don't think they're going to be so crazy about the high-heeled shoes either."

"It isn't fair," I said. "Some people have sophisticated families and go to Europe and live in houses with enough closets. They're bound to be sophisticated."

"Would they like to adopt me?" Andrea asked, and moved over to check the temperature on the oven. "I could use some more closets, and I wouldn't turn down a trip to Europe."

"Stand in line," I said. "Can't you think of any other way I could be sophisticated?"

"You could read sophisticated books," Andrea said, putting the veal in the oven. "You still reading Nancy Drew?"

I shook my head.

"Good," she said. "How about *The Bell Jar?* You read that yet?"

"What is that?" I asked.

"It's a very sophisticated book," Andrea said, wiping her hands on her apron. "That creep Harvey used to hate it, but I must have read it twice a year all the time I was in college. You'll love it."

"You think so?" I asked, not much caring. The important thing was that it make me sophisticated, not that I love it.

"Oh, sure," Andrea said. "It's all about pain and breakdowns and suicide. Fabulous book."

"Sounds great," I said, wishing I hadn't stopped reading Nancy Drew quite so fast.

"I'll get it for you right now," Andrea said. "Between that and my cooking, you'll be so sophisticated you won't know what to do with yourself. Wait there, and after I get it, we can talk about sophisticated music too."

"Great," I said. Maybe if I hummed some sophisticated music around Jessica that would do the trick and I wouldn't have to read the book too.

Andrea scurried out of the kitchen, and I started stacking up dishes in the sink when the phone rang. I picked it up right away.

"Hi, Cathy," Mary Kay said. "How're you?"

"I'm fine," I said. "Did you call Francie?"

"Yeah, I did," she said. "She says you owe her a letter."

"Oh, I guess I do," I said. "Things have been so busy. You know how it is."

"Don't apologize to me," Mary Kay said. "You don't owe me a letter."

"That's right," I said and giggled. "Oh, one of my new friends wanted to know how the boys are at St. Theresa's."

"I guess they're okay," Mary Kay replied. "I miss the kids I used to go to school with. My mom says if I still don't like St. Theresa's by the end of the school year, I can go to the junior high. Wouldn't that be great?"

"It sure would," I said. It would be wonderful to have Mary Kay back. She was sure to love Jessica and fit right in.

"Anyway, I thought maybe if I got to meet those new friends of yours, and maybe my mother could meet them too somehow, she'd see they were okay and just maybe she'd let me go to the junior high second semester," Mary Kay said. "It's a real long shot, but I've been crying a lot lately and she says she hates to see me this unhappy."

"That would be wonderful," I said.

"So you think maybe you could work it out?" Mary Kay asked. "I could come over to your house over the weekend, and you could have the other girls over, and then my mom could pick me up early, and she could meet them all. What do you think?"

"Sure," I said, and then in a sudden awful moment, I remembered what Mary Kay looked like. She was three inches shorter than I am, and really scrawny, and she wore her hair in braids still. Besides, she was ten. How was I going to convince Jessica I was sophisticated if she saw my old best friend was ten going on seven?

And it wasn't like Mary Kay's trick was going to work. I knew her mother well enough to know Mary Kay was just dreaming. Besides, Jessica was probably just the sort of person Mary Kay's mother was trying to keep her from. Older and sophisticated, like I wanted to be. No braids.

"Oh, thanks, Cathy," Mary Kay said. "When should I come? How many of your friends do you think you could have over? Make sure they all behave themselves, okay?"

"Wait a second," I said. "How about if it's just Libby?"

"I don't understand," Mary Kay said. "My mother already knows Libby."

"But she's so nice," I said. "And if your mother sees too many of us all at once she might panic."

"I thought you had lots of nice friends," Mary Kay said. "All those girls with the fancy names."

"They're not really close friends yet," I said. "And your mother wouldn't like them anyway, I'm sure. Why take chances?"

"Just Libby, huh?" Mary Kay said. "How about if your mother talked to my mother, too, and told her how junior high is really okay?"

"Sure," I said. "My mother likes talking to your mother. And junior high really is okay."

"All right," Mary Kay said. "Why don't you find out when would be good for Libby, and I'll come over then too. And talk to your mother too. Don't forget, Cathy. This is really important."

"I promise I won't," I said, and I looked up and noticed Andrea standing in the kitchen doorway, "I've got to go now," I told Mary Kay. "I'll talk to you later."

"Bye, Cathy," she said, and we hung up.

"I brought you the book," Andrea said. "And a couple of other sophisticated books I love. You may have a little trouble with the Virginia Woolf, but she is absolutely the most sophisticated writer in the whole world."

"Thanks, Andrea," I said, taking the pile of books from her. "This is really nice of you."

"If you want to be sophisticated, I'd be delighted to help," Andrea replied. "I really want to help you, Cathy, to give you the love and support no one gave me at your age. Except Mom and Dad, and they didn't really know what they were doing. It's always roughest on the firstborn."

"The youngest have it rough too," I said. "These books look terrific." Actually they looked terrifying.

"I don't know how you feel about poetry," Andrea said. "But it's very sophisticated stuff."

"That's right," I said. "You were supposed to tell me about sophisticated music."

But before she had the chance to, the doorbell rang. I put the books down on the kitchen counter and went to the front hall to answer it.

It was Libby. "Hi, Cathy," she said. "I hope you don't mind my just dropping in like this."

"No, that's fine," I said. "I wanted to talk to you anyway, to see if you could come over for a visit during the weekend. Saturday afternoon maybe?"

"Sure," Libby said, and gave me a big smile. "I'd really like that."

"Great," I said. "Want to come in?"

"Yeah," Libby said, and she followed me into the living room. It was awfully messy, especially compared to the way her house looked. I hoped Jessica never dropped in unexpectedly, at least not until we got some cleaning help.

"I had a really good time at your house," I said, grabbing a pile of newspapers off the sofa and dropping them onto the floor. Libby sat next to me on the sofa. "Thanks for having the sleepover."

"I had a good time too," Libby said. "But that's kind of what I wanted to talk to you about."

"You're not still mad?" I asked.

Libby laughed. "Of course not," she said. "It worked out fine. Don't worry."

"Good," I said, and turned around on the sofa so I'd be facing her. This sounded serious and I wanted to give her my complete attention.

"It's about your brother," Libby said.

"Mark?" I asked. "What about him?"

"Not Mark," Libby said. "Paul. The one you won't let Michelle meet."

"I don't know why anyone would want to meet him," I grumbled.

"It's just I was talking to my mother about it, and she said maybe there was something wrong with Paul, you know, like he had a problem or something, and maybe you were shy about it," Libby said all in a rush. "Like it would make a difference, which of course it wouldn't, so I thought I should discuss it with you when you were alone, in case you were embarrassed."

"Paul doesn't have a problem," I said. "He's just strange."

"How strange?" Libby asked. "I don't want to seem pushy. . . ."

"The thing is he dances," I said. If I had to tell one of them, it might as well be Libby. She, at least, was nice enough to be concerned. "He dances ballet." I made a face to show Libby what I thought of that.

"He does?" Libby asked. "He takes ballet lessons?"

"All the time," I said. "He wants to be a great ballet dancer. He's always practicing. It's a real bore."

"I think that sounds interesting," Libby said. "I used to take ballet lessons, but I wasn't very good at it. Is Paul good?"

"He thinks he is," I replied. "I guess he is. He sure practices enough. And that's all he ever talks about. And some people might think that's weird, you know."

"Oh, I see," Libby said. "Well, I don't think it's weird at all. I'd like to see him dance."

"Really?" I said.

"Sure," she replied. "Maybe he'll be famous someday, and I'll be able to say I knew him when."

"He's having a dance recital in two weeks," I said. "Andrea was supposed to go, only a friend of hers is getting married so she's going to be out of town instead. If you really want to come. . . ."

"I'd love to," Libby said. "Make sure to ask Paul for the ticket for me. He might give it to somebody else."

"That's no problem," I said. "Nobody else ever wants to go. But I'll check anyway."

"Thanks," Libby said. "Wow, I just come over here and I end up with two invitations."

We talked for a while longer and then Libby had to go home. When I saw she was halfway down the block, I closed the front door and went back to the kitchen to get the books Andrea was lending me.

"I like Libby," Andrea said. She was peeling the carrots. I took the knife off the counter and started slicing them for her.

"I like her too," I said. "But she isn't Jessica."

"Is Jessica why you want to be sophisticated?" she asked.

"Yeah, sort of," I admitted. "She said she'd like me better if I was sophisticated."

"Why don't you show her just how sophisticated you really are," Andrea suggested. "Invite her for dinner one night. I'll cook a meal that'll age both of you ten years. How's that?"

"I don't know," I said. "The house is such a mess. And Paul is weird. And I don't think Mom and Dad are much like her parents."

"We can clean the house," Andrea replied. "And I'll make sure Paul is on his best behavior. And Mom and Dad are really good people. Besides, if you want Jessica to like you, you've got to show her you like her. Invite her for dinner, so she'll get the chance to know you better. It works every time."

"You really think so?" I asked, trying to picture Jessica here, eating in my house, which was suddenly absolutely clean with brand-new furniture.

"I'm sure of it," Andrea said. "You just let me know what day she's coming, and I'll make up a menu that would do New York City proud."

"Great," I said, and I felt good just thinking about it. With the books and the music and the food, I'd be sophisticated and Jessica would be sure to like me the best.

Chapter 10

I nearly went crazy waiting for Mom to come home from the library so I could ask her if Jessica could come to dinner. She was later than usual, or at least it felt that way, but eventually she came and she said of course Jessica could come, there was always room for one more.

So then I had to figure out how to invite Jessica without everybody else knowing about it, and wanting to come too. I'd seen Amy in action, and I didn't want to take any chances. The easiest thing, I decided, was to call Jessica on the phone, and invite her that way. Which was when I realized that even though I'd given Jessica my phone number twice, she'd never given me hers.

"Where's the phone book?" I screeched, and Andrea shouted back, "In the hall closet."

So I ran to the hall closet, and sure enough, on the floor, was the phone book. I'll never understand why things end up where they do in our house. There's no phone in the hall closet, after all.

It turned out there were a bunch of Greens living in our town, and I didn't think any of them were Jessica's. No Doctor Greens, for one thing, and no Greens with addresses like the one I was pretty sure Jessica had.

What if she had an unlisted number? I'd never be able to invite her!

But part of me calmed down right away. Even if Jessica had an unlisted number, which she'd never remembered to give me, there were plenty of people who must know what the number was. Libby was bound to have it. I'd just have to call Libby and ask for Jessica's number and lie about why I needed it.

I didn't much like the idea of lying to Libby, but I didn't want to hurt her feelings by telling her I was inviting Jessica to dinner and not her. I hadn't wanted to hurt Mary Kay's feelings, either, telling her she was too babyish to play with most of my friends. I was really becoming a very considerate person, which was probably just a step behind sophisticated. A really grown-up person was bound to be considerate, I told myself, as I dialed Libby's number. I was surprised to discover I knew it already. I hadn't realized I'd called her that often.

After I'd said hello to Libby's mother, Libby got on the phone. "I'm glad you called," she said. "I forgot to write down the English assignment."

So I gave it to her. Then we talked for ten minutes about all kinds of stuff. We were just about to hang up when I realized I'd forgotten to ask for Jessica's number. So I did.

Libby didn't even ask me why I needed it. She just recited it to me, reminded me to ask Paul for the dance recital ticket, and said she'd see me in school tomorrow.

So we hung up, and I didn't have to lie at all. I felt better after that, even though I'd have lied for Libby's own good.

My fingers trembled when I dialed Jessica's number, and I thought I might die if her mother answered, but fortunately I recognized Jessica's voice saying hello. I tried to make sure mine didn't crack as I said hello back.

"Who is this?" she asked.

"It's me, Cathy," I gulped out.

"Oh," Jessica said. "Hello, Cathy."

"Hi," I said. "Look, Jessica, I was wondering if you could come here for supper

Friday night. My sister doesn't cook very big meals but they're really very good. Can you come?"

"Let me check with my mother," Jessica said, and I could hear her putting the telephone down. I imagined what her house looked like, all white and glistening and clean. Even the phone was white, I decided. They probably even had a white telephone book, right where the white telephone was.

"Mom says it's fine," Jessica said a minute or so later. "What time do you want me to come?"

"We have supper around seven," I said. "Want to come over after school? You can walk home with me."

"I can't," Jessica said. "I have piano lessons on Fridays. But I can come over after that, and be at your house around six. How's that?"

"Fine," I said. "And then my mother can drive you home."

"Very good," Jessica said. "Thank you for inviting me, Cathy."

"Thank you," I said and hung up. I couldn't believe it. Jessica had accepted my invitation. She really was going to come over. And I had almost four whole days to get the house completely clean and neat and perfect. I wondered how many closets we could build in four days.

"She's coming!" I shouted to the world. "Mom, we have to clean the house this week. Okay? I'll clean every single room but everybody has to promise to make sure things stay clean."

"Don't you dare clean my room," Paul said. "You'll just mess up my system."

"I wouldn't touch your room with a ten-foot pole," I declared. "Just keep your door closed, okay?"

"If you promise to keep your mouth closed," Paul said.

"What's the excitement?" Dad asked, coming into the house. He tried to hang his coat on the coat rack, but it slipped off. So he picked it up and carried it to the living room, where he flung it on the back of a chair. Then he dropped his briefcase on the sofa, loosened his tie, and threw his jacket on the easy chair.

It was a good thing I liked a challenge, I told myself. Either that or we'd have to keep the doors closed to every room so Jessica wouldn't see them.

But it turned out that my family cooperated in keeping the place neat between Monday and Friday. People started hanging their coats up as soon as they came in, and briefcases got put on desks. Paul kept his door closed, and Andrea helped me vacuum and sweep and scrub.

"Drudgery," she informed me as we polished the kitchen floor. "Houses were put on earth by men to keep women enslaved to them. If that creep Harvey had had his way, I never would have left the apartment."

I knew it was drudgery too, but it was important drudgery. There was no way my house would ever look as good as I knew Jessica's must, but at least I wanted it to look as good as it possibly could. And by Thursday night the place really did look good. Mom even offered to hire me to be her housecleaner, but after a few days of cleaning, I decided I didn't want to do it for a living, so I turned her down.

I got home from school Friday with the biggest stomachache of my life. It had been murder all week long making sure nobody else knew that Jessica was coming for dinner. Not that Jessica was mentioning it to anyone, not even me. But I was sure I'd slip up and say something to somebody. So the whole week I'd had to watch what I was saying, and make up stuff too, since I didn't want to have to explain why I was cleaning house, which was just about all I was doing.

And then on Friday, I was convinced Jessica had forgotten about having dinner with me, and I had to figure out a way to get her alone so I could remind her. It wasn't easy, since Jessica was always surrounded by a group of kids. But finally I saw her alone for a moment in the hallway and I ran over to her, not caring if I looked sophisticated while I ran.

"Do you remember about tonight?" I asked her.

"Certainly," she said and smiled at me. "I'll be there around six."

She hadn't forgotten! It must mean a lot to her if she hadn't forgotten, and I hadn't mentioned it to her all week long. I laughed at myself for having worried about it and kept on running to my next class.

I went home right after school and gave the house an inspection to make sure it was spotlessly clean. It really wasn't, but it was as clean as I could hope to make it. I threw some extra junk into a closet, slammed the door closed, and went to the kitchen to see how Andrea was doing.

"Don't look," she told me. "I want the meal to be a surprise for you."

"It smells nice," I said.

"It should," she said. "I've been working on it all day long."

"You're really so great," I said, and I gave her the biggest hug I'd ever given her in my whole life. "I couldn't have done this without you. Thank you, Andrea, forever."

"I've had fun too," she said. "And it was important to teach you about how terrible housework really is. I guess you haven't had time to read any of those books I loaned you."

"Not really," I said. Actually I'd picked up *The Bell Jar* and tried reading it, but I'd gotten bored by page two. I didn't want to tell Andrea that. And next week, when I didn't have Jessica's dinner to look forward to, I might enjoy it.

Right when I was starting to go really crazy waiting for Jessica to arrive, the phone rang. I just knew it was Jessica calling to cancel, so I answered the phone myself, absolutely swearing not to cry, no matter what.

But it wasn't Jessica. It was Mary Kay. I was so relieved I nearly started crying anyway.

"Hi," she said. "I just figured I'd call up and remind you about tomorrow."

"What about tomorrow?" I asked her.

"My visit," she said. "Honestly, Cathy, I didn't think you'd really need reminding."

"Then why did you call to remind me?" I asked her, frantic to get off the phone. What if Jessica were trying to call to say she needed a lift over? Mary Kay had no sense of timing.

"It was just an excuse," Mary Kay replied. "So what's up?"

"Nothing," I said. "Look Mary Kay, I really can't talk to you now. We're expecting company, and I have to help out."

"Who's coming?" she asked. "Anybody I know?"

"No," I said. "I'll see you tomorrow, okay?"

"Okay," Mary Kay said. "Boy, you sure have gotten grouchy. Don't you like who-ever's coming?"

"I like them," I said. "It's just I have to keep the phone free in case of a call."

"Well, okay," she said. "Why didn't you tell me that?"

I honestly thought I had. "See you tomorrow," I said, and hung up before Mary Kay had a chance to analyze my company even longer. I only prayed Jessica hadn't been trying to reach me.

Waiting for Jessica after that was agony, but eventually she did arrive. I took her coat and bag and hung them up in the hall closet so she couldn't see what a mess it was. Then I introduced her to Mom and Andrea and Paul, since Dad wasn't home from work yet. Jessica shook all their hands and told them it was nice to meet them. I wished I could talk like that to strangers.

We all sat in the living room, and Mom and Jessica chatted about stuff like what her parents did and what she liked to do. I went to the kitchen to check on Andrea but she shooed me out and said things were under control. I just wished my heart would stop thumping.

I went back to the living room in time to hear Jessica say, "This is a very nice living room. It's very homey."

"We don't usually have the TV set in the living room," I blurted. "It's usually in Andrea's room, but Andrea's in there now so we moved it here. Everything's a little bit different because Andrea's here."

"I'll say," Paul muttered. "Look, if you don't mind, I think I'll go upstairs and practice before supper."

"Practice what?" Jessica asked. "If you don't mind my asking."

"Dance," Paul replied. "I have a recital in a week."

I held my breath for a record amount of time. Now Jessica knew. What if she thought it was really weird that Paul danced? Would she refuse to have dinner here?

"What sort of dance?" Jessica asked, to make matters worse.

"Ballet," Paul replied.

"Really?" Jessica said. "That's fascinating. Who do you study with?"

"Dariel this year," Paul said. "But I have a really good shot at School of the American Ballet next year."

"That's fabulous," Jessica said. "I tried out for Dariel but I didn't make it. You must be great to study with him."

"It's easier if you're a man," Paul said. "They're always looking for good male dancers."

"But you still have to be good," Jessica said. "Are you serious about the ballet?"

"Ballet is my life," Paul declared, looking as dumb as he always does when he says stuff like that.

"I'm so envious," Jessica said. "I wish I had that sort of dedication. My problem is I'm just a little bit good at a lot of things, so I never settle on just one to get very good at."

"You need that sort of dedication if you're going to make it in the arts," Paul said. "I've always known I wanted to be a ballet dancer. Ever since I saw my first *Nutcracker*."

"I knew it then too," Jessica said. "But I knew I wanted to be a great musician when I went to my first *Peter and the Wolf*. And I wanted to be a great painter after I saw my first Renoir."

"Where have you been hiding this girl?" Paul asked me. "Usually Cathy's friends are so childish," he told Jessica. "Always giggling about something. They've never even heard of Renoir."

I didn't know how to feel after that, happy that Paul liked Jessica so much, or mad that he put down all my other friends. So I just grunted, but they didn't even hear me.

"I'm having a dance recital," Paul said. "The one I mentioned. I had to beg Dariel for an extra ticket for Andrea, but then she decided she couldn't come. Why don't you come instead, Jessica?"

"I'd love to," Jessica replied. "I'll get to see what I've been missing because Dariel wouldn't accept me."

"He is very good," Paul said. "But I'm ready to move on. He agrees."

"You mean you want to come?" I asked Jessica. "Really?"

"Of course," Jessica said. "I really don't understand why you've been keeping us from meeting Paul, Cathy. He's wonderful."

My mouth was open wide enough to ram a tractor trailer through it. It was a good thing Dad walked in then, because it gave my jaws an excuse to move. I introduced Dad to Jessica, who shook his hand and told him what a fine time she was having discussing the ballet with Paul. I just stared at her. Jessica wanted to go to the dance recital. She wanted to do something with my family. She liked Paul. It was really too amazing.

"Dinner's ready!" Andrea called out to us from the dining room.

"It smells wonderful," Mom said. "What have you prepared for us tonight Andrea?"

"Salmon in raspberry sauce," Andrea called out. "It's my own recipe."

"It sounds delicious," Jessica said, and walked with Paul into the dining room.

"Oh, Lord," Dad muttered to Mom, as the two of them walked in.

I followed them all into the dining room. I tended to agree with Dad about what dinner would be like, but the important thing was Jessica thought it sounded good. Jessica liked my family, my house, my food. Jessica was going with me to the dance recital.

And it wasn't until then that I remembered that I was supposed to ask Paul if Libby could use the ticket. How could I tell Libby that Paul had given her ticket away?

Chapter 11

It was terrible.

All Saturday afternoon, when I should have been having a good time with Libby and Mary Kay, all I could think about was how I could convince Libby that she didn't want to go to the dance recital.

I tried to bring it up a couple of times, but then I thought Mary Kay's feelings would be hurt because I hadn't asked her. Not that she'd ever enjoyed Paul's recitals when she was my best friend. But I was getting so considerate about people's feelings, I didn't know anymore what people would get hurt by. I was starting to think everybody could be hurt by everything, and that would include Libby too, whom I didn't want to hurt, but I had to make sure she didn't go to the recital.

As it happened, she brought it up in front of Mary Kay. "I have a terrible problem about next weekend," she announced.

"What kind of problem?" I asked, figuring it couldn't be worse than mine.

"What about next weekend?" Mary Kay asked.

"Cathy invited me to Paul's dance recital," Libby said. "But I might have to go to a wedding instead."

"Yuck," Mary Kay said. "I used to go to those dumb recitals all the time. I hope you have to go to the wedding."

At least Mary Kay's feelings weren't hurt. Now that I thought about it, I'd asked her to recitals twice the year before, and both times she'd turned me down because she disliked them so much. I should have known she wouldn't mind. But there was so much to know if you were going to be sophisticated and have lots of friends. I didn't know how Jessica managed it.

"You don't understand," Libby said and sighed. "My father hates all that side of his family. Whenever we have to go to one of those things he gets mean for an entire week. Mom says she RSVPed that we're coming, but she doesn't really know if we are, since Dad might decide at the last minute that he hates those people and doesn't want to go to their stupid wedding, and then Mom'll call them and cancel out.

Dad won't care what they think of us, because he hates them so much. Oh, I hope we don't have to go. He just screams for no reason at all for days after he sees his family."

"That is terrible," Mary Kay said. "I hope you don't have to go."

"So does Mom," Libby said. "She doesn't understand why Dad told her we should go in the first place, but they're his family, so she figured if he said we should go, we should. So I won't know for a while about the dance recital. Is that a problem?"

"I don't think so," I said, thinking it wasn't a problem — it was a solution. "If you can't use the ticket, we can always find somebody else."

"Don't even think about asking me," Mary Kay said.

"I wasn't," I told her, happy to be telling the truth without hurting people's feelings.

It was right then that I started thinking about concentrating all my psychic energies on getting Libby's father to decide to go to the wedding. Andrea was very big on psychic energies, and how if you concentrated hard enough, you could get things to happen.

"If I concentrate hard enough, that creep Harvey'll drop dead," she told me one day as we chopped mushrooms. "But since I don't really want him to die, I'm concentrating on his slipping on a piece of ice and breaking both his legs. And his arms. That should be enough."

As far as I knew, Harvey was fine, but there wasn't any ice yet, not even in Boston. And I liked the idea of getting what I wanted through psychic energy. I'd been concentrating a lot on getting Jessica to like me, and it seemed to be working. So now all I had to do was concentrate on Libby's father, so he'd decide to go, and then Libby wouldn't know I hadn't remembered to ask Paul, and Jessica would go to the dance recital, and nobody's feelings would get hurt.

So instead of thinking about Libby and Mary Kay and the good time we were having, I concentrated on Libby's father instead. And when Mary Kay's mother came over, I didn't concentrate on trying to convince her to let Mary Kay go to the junior high. Instead I thought about how families should get together for weddings, and what fun weddings were, and families were, and how families were simply the most important things in the world. I hardly even noticed when Mary Kay gave me a fingers-crossed wave goodbye. And even though Libby stayed for another hour or so, and we talked about all kinds of stuff, I just pretended to listen. Instead I pictured her father over and over again, and the wedding.

I guess Libby could see my mind wasn't on her, because she left sooner than she'd planned. I wasn't that sorry to see her go, since I knew it would be easier to concentrate if I was alone.

I concentrated all day Sunday too, except when I was eating or doing homework. I bet nobody ever concentrated as hard as I did, not even Andrea. I could practically feel my thoughts going to Libby's father.

Then I realized I didn't have to concentrate all that hard. Libby's father had decided they were going to the wedding; Libby was just hoping he'd change his mind. All I had to do was make sure he stuck to what he'd originally decided. When I realized that I started concentrating just a little bit less.

Monday morning I found Libby walking to school and we walked the last couple of blocks together. "I have bad news," she said, and she looked miserable.

"What?" I asked, trying to keep the excitement from my voice.

"Dad says we're definitely going to the wedding," Libby said. "It was awful. He and Mom got into a big fight over it. They were screaming and yelling for hours. It was terrible."

"Do you think they're going to get a divorce?" I asked. I hadn't meant my psychic energies to do that.

Libby gave me a funny look. "Of course not," she said. "They just fight sometimes. Don't your parents ever fight?"

"Sure," I said. "But you made it sound so bad, that's all."

"It was bad," Libby said. "And it's going to be bad all week long and then it's going to be even worse next week. You should see what my father is like after he's had to see his family."

"But he'll get over it," I said, trying to cheer her up. "And your parents aren't going to get a divorce or anything, and think of all the good food you'll get to eat at the wedding. And you really wouldn't have enjoyed the dance recital, so you won't be missing anything. It isn't so bad really."

"Yes, it is," Libby said. "I don't want to put you on the spot, but do you think you can hold on to my ticket, just in case? I don't think Dad is going to change his mind, but he might."

"Oh, sure, don't worry," I said, knowing my psychic energies would keep that from happening. "That's nothing. Are you going to buy a new dress for the wedding?"

"Mom says we are," Libby replied. "She says if we're both going to be stuck with Dad for the next few days, the least we can do is get some new clothes out of it."

"That sounds like fun," I said, but I wasn't listening anymore. It was amazing what you could do with psychic energies. Of course I didn't want Libby to be miserable, but that wasn't my fault. I just wanted to spare her feelings and that I'd managed to do. She'd never know I'd forgotten her and that Jessica had gotten her ticket. Everybody would be happy. It really couldn't have worked out better.

So all week long I was happy. Libby was kind of down, and a couple of times she snapped at people and had to apologize right away, but I always forgave her. I was so happy I could have forgiven anybody anything. I didn't mind that Andrea's cooking was getting stranger and stranger, or that Paul was even more obsessed than usual, and you couldn't even say hello to him without his scowling and telling you to shut up. I forgave Mom and Dad for letting the house get messy again, even though I knew I'd have to straighten things out again, so Jessica wouldn't be horrified if she came over to our house the night of the recital. And I especially forgave Jessica who never even mentioned the dance recital. She just didn't like to mention things. I'd learned that the week before. She knew what good stuff was going to happen, and she didn't like other people to feel left out by discussing it where they might hear her. And if she didn't call me at night to talk about all the good stuff, it was probably because she lost my phone number. Or maybe she was just shy about calling. Or maybe her parents let her make only one phone call a week, and that had to be to her grandmother. There were lots of good reasons why she wasn't calling, so I didn't let it bother me. Not when I was so happy.

I convinced Mom that I should have a new outfit to wear to the recital, and she let me go shopping with Andrea, who had much more sophisticated taste in clothes than Mom did. Andrea and I shopped for hours, trying to find just the right thing. We finally settled on a navy blue dress with white lace piping.

"Very simple," Andrea declared, as I modeled it for her. "Very chic."

I would have preferred something black and low cut, but I knew there were limits to what I could get away with. And at least the dress wasn't red check or something else babyish, like Mom would have insisted on.

Libby and I walked home together after school on Friday. I tried to hide how happy I was from her, since she looked like the world was about to end.

"It's only a wedding," I said, trying to comfort her. "Your father'll get over it."

"I know," she said. "But it's just been horrible all week long. Dad snaps at everything. He knows he's made a mistake, and he can't figure out what to do about it."

"His family can't be that bad," I said. "I'll bet you'll have a wonderful time."

"Never." Libby kicked at some leaves on the ground. They gave off a nice crackling sound, but she didn't seem to notice. She stared at the sidewalk, and kept walking and kicking, walking and kicking, walking and kicking.

I felt a little bit bad then, like somehow I'd made her father decide to go to the wedding and make everybody miserable. But I knew that was crazy. All I'd done was concentrate my psychic energies. Dr. Katz was the one who'd done the actual deciding, and he'd decided before I ever even knew about it. There was no way I was responsible. It was my being so considerate that made me feel bad about Libby. I should feel good that I felt bad. It was qualities like being considerate that were going to make me Jessica's best friend.

"Oh, well," Libby said when we got to my corner. "I'd ask you to come home with me, but I wouldn't do that to my worst enemy."

"That's okay," I said. "I'll see you on Monday."

"Tuesday," she said. "Monday's Columbus Day. I'll talk to you Sunday to see how the dance recital went."

"Fine," I said. "And cheer up. It's just a wedding."

"I'll be okay," she said, and gave me the saddest smile. I really got mad at her father then, for making my friend so unhappy. But there was nothing I could do about that, except smile back at Libby.

"Talk to you soon," I said and started walking off. It made no sense at all for me to be feeling quite so upset about Libby, but I did. If only she hadn't looked quite so unhappy. Maybe I shouldn't have concentrated my psychic energies quite that hard. Maybe I could have asked if Paul could try to get an extra ticket for the stupid recital. Not that what I'd done made any difference. But just in case it had, I shouldn't have done it that well. It was all very confusing.

I hardly ate any supper that night, which nobody minded since it meant there was more for everyone else. Not that Paul ate all that much, either. He went around all evening long with a glazed look in his eyes. I don't think he even knew we were in the same house with him. I thought about asking him if there would have been an extra ticket, but there was no point, since he'd had to beg to get the one extra. Besides, when he got that dedicated, it was always better to avoid him.

I didn't sleep well that night either, but I figured it was all the excitement. After all Jessica and I were going to be going to the recital together. I was especially happy that we were going to do something without Amy and Michelle tagging along. I sometimes had the feeling Jessica might be a little nicer to me if Amy and Michelle weren't around. Someday, when it was just Jessica and Libby and me, things would really be perfect.

But until then it was enough that Jessica would be alone with me. And Dad said that after the performance we'd all get ice-cream sundaes. Jessica loved ice cream, so she was bound to enjoy that. And when she'd spent more time with me and my family, she would be sure to realize how wonderful we all were. She seemed to feel that way about Paul already, and he was the least wonderful member of my family by a long shot.

I just wished I didn't keep having dreams about Libby. I kept dreaming she was at the wedding and crying. I woke up a lot, wondering if she was having dreams about me. I hoped not. I was so happy that I'd be bound to be happy in her dreams, and that would only make her sadder. It really wasn't fair.

The next morning was real zooey at our house. Andrea hogged the bathroom for hours before she decided she was ready for the wedding she was going to. She was planning to stay overnight with friends of hers, so she packed an overnight bag, and kept running back to the bathroom to get deodorant and toothpaste. Finally she was ready, and Dad drove her to the train station, where she could get a train to the city, and then another train to the town where the wedding was being held. Ordinarily I would have envied her missing the recital, but instead I felt sorry for her. She wasn't going to spend the evening with Jessica.

Then Paul decided he had to go to the studio and rehearse, so Mom drove him over. He announced that he wouldn't bother coming home before the recital, which made me very happy. His scowling was making me nervous.

So I was alone when the phone rang. I picked it up right away, thinking it was Jessica. But instead it was Mary Kay.

"How're things going?" she asked me.

"You know, you always call at exactly the wrong times," I said. "You have a real gift for that, Mary Kay."

"There doesn't seem to be a right time with you anymore," she replied. "Whenever I call, you're busy doing something."

"I'm busy," I admitted. "I'm a busy person. What's wrong with that?"

"You never used to be too busy for me," she said. "There was a time you would have called me right after I got home to see what my mother said about me going to the junior high."

This was not the time for Mary Kay to tell me she was going to join me at the junior high. Maybe after Jessica and I became best friends, I might be able to convince Jessica to overlook Mary Kay's babyish appearance, but not now. I couldn't believe Mary Kay's parents might actually be doing this to me.

"Are you going to be able to go?" I croaked.

"Not until next year," Mary Kay said. "But Mom and Dad both agreed if I still wanted to by next year, I could. I was hoping for better, but that isn't too bad. And maybe I can get them to change their minds and let me go next semester."

"Sure," I said, my mind already a million miles off. "That's great, Mary Kay. You'll like junior high."

"I think I may like it less than I thought I was going to," she said. "Goodbye, Cathy. Give me a call when you remember how to listen."

"What do you mean?" I asked.

"You're right," she said. "You never call anymore, do you?" And then she hung up on me.

Before I had a chance to figure out why Mary Kay was so upset, the phone rang again. This time it was Libby.

"I have great news!" she cried happily into the telephone. "Dad changed his mind at the very last minute."

"What?" I asked, not understanding.

"He says he's crazy to go to the wedding," Libby said. "He says he hates his family and Mom was right and he's sorry he made us all miserable all week long and he was miserable too, and he doesn't want to be miserable next week also, so we're not going. Isn't that great?"

"It sure is," I said, genuinely happy for Libby.

"So now I can go to the dance recital," Libby said. "What time do you want me to get to your house?"

I actually gasped.

"Cathy?" Libby said. "Are you still there?"

"Yeah," I said. "Libby, you can't go to the recital. I don't have a ticket for you." I couldn't think of a lie to tell her, so I prayed she wouldn't ask me why.

"Why?" she asked.

"Well, you told me you weren't going to go," I said defensively. I don't know why I felt that way, since none of this was my fault. "Paul gave your ticket away, without asking me."

"Oh," Libby said. "I told you to ask him to hold it for me."

"I forgot," I admitted. "And I can't get another ticket. If you'd just called a couple of minutes earlier, I could have asked Paul, but he just walked out, and I don't dare call him at the studio. I'm sorry, Libby."

"No, that's okay," she said. "It isn't your fault. Paul gave the ticket away. You didn't. I just wish you hadn't forgotten."

"You wouldn't have liked it anyway," I

said. "They're really awful, just like Mary Kay said."

"I know," Libby said. "It just sounded like fun, doing something with your family. I like your family."

"It won't even be all my family," I said. "Andrea's already left for her wedding."

Libby laughed. "Maybe I should go with her. I seem to be short one wedding."

I laughed too, but it didn't sound very real to me. "I'm sorry," I said. "Really I am, Libby."

"I know," she said. "Oh, well. Dad said he was going to take Mom and me out to dinner to make up for the way he's been behaving. And that should be fun."

"More fun than the stupid recital," I said. "I wish I could go with you."

"Some other time," Libby said. "Well, have a good time tonight, Cathy."

"You too," I said and hung up the phone. I'd been so sure I was going to have a good time too, when I thought Libby was going to be miserable.

Even though I knew lying was wrong, I wasn't quite sure why I should feel bad when I wasn't lying all that much, and besides I was doing all the lying to make sure nobody's feelings were going to be hurt. That was the right sort of lying, if there was a right sort of lying, which I certainly hoped there was.

I also hoped that someday I would be sophisticated enough to understand friendship, because I didn't like the idea of being this confused for the rest of my life.

Chapter 12

I never enjoy Paul's recitals much, but this
one I had been sure would be different because I'd be seeing it with Jessica. The
funny thing was Jessica obviously did enjoy it. She hardly blinked her eyes the
entire time. Sometimes she even nodded,
like someone had just made a good point.

Mom and Dad sat there and looked proud
every time Paul danced, which was a lot. I
guess he was the best. At least he got the
most applause, but no one gave him a
bouquet of flowers, like they gave to the
girl dancers. I have to admit there were a
couple of moments there when I was proud
of him too. He leaped around the stage a
lot, and it looked like he was flying. He got
a lot of applause then, and I clapped too,
real loud. And he looked handsome at cur-
tain calls, not like my creepy big brother
at all. More like a real ballet dancer. Mom

got a little teary then, and Dad murmured, "He really is something" to all of us. And I knew what he meant.

Afterward we went backstage, which was a madhouse with dancers being hugged by parents and friends and other dancers, and pictures being taken, and Mr. Dariel running around telling everybody what they'd done wrong. Only he patted Paul on the back, and then hugged him, and said he'd done brilliantly. Paul stood two inches taller after that, at least until he saw all of us. Then he just grinned and looked like my brother again, only nicer than usual.

"You were terrific!" I squealed and hugged him. I never hug Paul, but it seemed the right thing to do.

"You were great, son," Dad said, and then Mom hugged him, and Dad hugged him, and pretty soon we were all hugging each other. Jessica stood to one side and watched us, and then she said, "You were fabulous Paul," and I could tell she meant it. I'd never seen her look that enthusiastic about anyone before, and for one moment I felt a terrible pang. But then I got happy and excited again. I felt proud too when other people, especially grown-ups, came to Paul and told him how good he'd been, and asked what his future plans were. Paul was always telling us how good he was, but it was nice to see other people thought so too.

"We're going out for ice cream," Dad told him. "Can you join us, Paul?"

"I'd love to, Dad, but we're having kind of a party here," Paul replied, and grinned at some strange guy who pounded him on the back. "I'll get a lift home later, okay?"

"Fine," Dad said. "We're very proud of you, you know."

"Yeah, I know," Paul said, and he looked the way he had when Mr. Dariel had praised him. Mom got teary again, so we left fast before she started sobbing.

"I wasn't about to sob," she informed us in the car. "You didn't have to worry."

"I was afraid I might," Dad said. "When did Paul get so good?"

"He's been working like a fiend," Mom replied. "Or hadn't you noticed?"

"Andrea's noticed," I said. "Paul is always kicking her out of her room so he can practice in there."

"Andrea understands," Mom said. "You know, she's become a pretty good cook."

Dad snorted. "How can you tell?" he asked. "The portions are so small the food's all gone by the time the platter gets to me."

"Oh, Walter," Mom said. "It isn't that

bad. And you yourself said yesterday that supper was particularly good."

"I'm just kidding," Dad said. "I really have no complaints about any of my children. They're all turning out just fine."

I glanced at Jessica to see how she was taking all this. But she was looking out the car window, and I couldn't be sure what she thought of my parents' conversation.

We got to Comptons pretty late, but the place was crowded anyway. We had to wait for a little while before we got a table, but eventually we got one near the player piano. The place was a lot different on a Saturday night than it was after school. There were grown-ups there, and lots of high school kids out on dates. Mrs. Compton was almost smiling, and the player piano was going. The place seemed a lot friendlier than usual, and I felt comfortable there, and happy. It had been a very nice evening, and now my parents were going to treat Jessica and me to sundaes. I didn't even worry about figuring out which was the most sophisticated kind of sundae to get. I was sticking with hot fudge.

Jessica still wasn't talking much, but I figured that was because of all the noise and excitement. She looked okay, not bored or mad or anything. And when my mother asked her some questions, she answered them the polite way she always did with grown-ups. I tried to get her to talk about some school stuff, but she kept her answers pretty short.

"I'm sorry," she finally said to me. "My mind is on the recital, and how good everybody was."

"Sure," I said, although I could hardly remember what the recital had been like anymore. I've been to so many of them over the years, that they all started looking alike to me after a while. Mostly I daydream during them, except when Paul is on stage. Then I pay attention. But I guess for Jessica it was something special because she didn't have to go time after time. Besides, she danced, so she knew what was going on. No wonder she was still thinking about it.

"Cathy!"

Even through the din, I could hear somebody calling my name. I turned around, and sure enough, standing by the entrance were Libby and her parents. I waved back at them, and then realized I was out with Jessica. I hadn't even gotten around to telling Libby that Jessica was the substitute for the recital, and of course I'd never told Jessica that Libby was originally supposed to go. My stomach sank while my arm kept waving.

Libby said something to her parents, and walked over to our table. I dreaded the moment when she saw I was with Jessica. I was right to dread it too. Libby stopped smiling as soon as Jessica turned around to face her. But then she smiled again, and I decided it was going to be okay. As far as Libby knew, she was the first choice, after all. I had nothing to apologize to her for, and she no reason to be upset.

"Hi, Jessica," she said. "Hi, Mr. and Mrs. Wakefield. How're you?"

"Fine, Libby," my mother said. "Are you with your parents?"

"They're waiting on line for a table," Libby said. "Boy, your sundaes look good."

"They taste that way too," Dad said. "Weren't you supposed to be out of town this weekend? I thought Cathy mentioned something about a wedding."

"We ended up not going," Libby said. "It's a long story. We went to the movies instead."

"I know a lot of weddings where everybody would have been better off going to the movies instead," Mom said. "Including the bride and groom."

"I think they went through with it,"

Libby said. "But my parents decided not to go. So to celebrate we had supper out and then went to the movies, and now we're having ice cream."

"We were at Paul's dance recital," I said, like Libby didn't know. "He was pretty good."

"He was wonderful," Mom said. "I'm sorry you didn't get to see him."

"Maybe some other time," Libby said. "Did you have a good time, Jessica?"

"I had a fine time," she said. "Paul really was excellent. I was very impressed."

"And Cathy was afraid it was going to be a disaster," Libby said and laughed. I didn't like the way she laughed at all.

"I think I see your parents waving at you," I said, hoping they would wave real fast.

Libby looked back there. Her parents were talking to each other and very obviously not waving. Parents never do what you want them to do when you want them to do it.

"Say, Jessica," Libby said. "What time do you want me to come over tomorrow?"

"Oh, I don't know," Jessica said, looking uncomfortable. "Maybe around five."

"That sounds good," Libby said. "And

should I bring my new Danny McQueen album?"

"What's going on?" I asked. Nobody had mentioned anything about going to Jessica's to me.

"Jessica's having a sleepover," Libby said. "Tomorrow night. There's no school Monday, so it's okay. Didn't you know about it?"

"No," I said, looking straight at Jessica. She kind of blushed and turned the other way.

"Oh," Libby said. "Oh, that's right. Jessica said you weren't invited. I forgot."

Suddenly I knew I was going to start crying in the middle of Comptons. "Uh, excuse me, everyone," I said. "I think I have to go to the ladies' room."

"Cathy?" Mom said, but she didn't try to stop me. I managed to get out from behind the table and inch my way to the ladies' room. It wasn't much of a ladies' room, but there was a door with a lock on it, and that was all I needed. I knew I couldn't cry for very long, since other people would want to use the room. But I also knew I needed a couple of minutes to realize what it meant that Jessica was having a sleepover and hadn't invited me.

The problem with realizing was that it

made me want to really cry. Because what it obviously meant was that after everything I'd done, Jessica still didn't like me. And there wasn't anything more I could do without practically killing myself to make her like me. I'd lied, I'd gone places I didn't like, I'd hurt my friends' feelings more than once, I'd pretended to like salmon with raspberry sauce, I'd acted interested in all kinds of stuff that bored me, and none of it had mattered. Jessica just flat out didn't like me and that was that.

There was a knock on the door. "Cathy, can I come in?" I heard a voice say. "It's me, Jessica."

It was Jessica! For a second, I let myself think there had been a mistake, of course I was invited, I was being so silly, there had been a misunderstanding. I wiped away a couple of tears, and unlocked the door.

"Hi," Jessica said and came in fast. "We don't have much time to talk, because other people need to use the ladies' room. They're using the men's room instead."

"Oh," I said.

"I just wanted to apologize," Jessica said. "I didn't think you'd ever hear about the sleepover."

"Sure," I said, determined not to let her see me cry.

"It's very hard for me to get my mother to agree to sleepover parties," Jessica said. "She doesn't much like it when my friends come over. The noise gives her a headache. But I'd been to one at Libby's, so of course I had to have Libby back over. That's only good manners."

I nodded. Nobody knew more about manners than Jessica.

"My mother said I could have three girls over," Jessica continued. "So naturally I asked Libby and Amy and Michelle. I would have asked you if my mother had said I could have four girls over. And then I didn't think Libby would be able to make it, because she said if you weren't invited, she didn't want to go, but I guess she changed her mind. Libby can be very strange sometimes. She's unpredictable, like her father. But I guess she changed her mind again. I'm sorry you can't come too."

I stared at Jessica for a long, horrible moment. That was the longest speech Jessica had ever made to me, and it was an explanation of why I couldn't go to her house. "You don't like me much, do you?" I asked, trying to sound like it didn't matter.

"Of course I like you," Jessica said, but I could see she was just being polite.

"No, you don't," I said, wishing I didn't like her, either.

"We don't have very much in common," Jessica said, in her best grown-up voice. "But I've always thought you were very nice."

"I've gone along with everything you've wanted to do," I said. "I've tried to be mature and sophisticated for you. I kept you from meeting my friend Mary Kay, because she's only ten. I kept coming to Comptons, even though I hate Mrs. Compton. I used all my psychic energies to convince Libby's father to go to the wedding. And it never mattered to you."

"I never asked you to do that stuff," Jessica said. "I never asked you to like me. You've been tagging after me ever since school started, Cathy. I never asked you to. You just did it."

"I did it because I thought you were special!" I cried.

"Well, I'm sorry," she said. "I never meant for you to get upset like this."

"No," I said. "I guess you never did. But I want you to know something."

"What?" Jessica said, and I could see fear in her eyes.

"I lied to you about that English test," I said. "I told you I got an 86, but I really got a 92."

"What?" Jessica asked. "Oh, that. That was ages ago."

"I've been meaning to tell you for a while now," I said. "I just kept forgetting."

Jessica licked her lips. "I really should be going now," she said. "So should you. If you want, I can join Libby and her parents and you can go back home with your parents and not worry about dropping me off."

"That's probably a good idea," I said. "Goodbye, Jessica."

Jessica gave a nervous little laugh. "You sound like it's the end of the world," she said. "I'll see you in school on Tuesday."

"Sure," I said. "See you there." I watched as she left the ladies' room. I didn't care that there were three people standing by the door, waiting for me to leave. I gave myself five minutes, and I cried hard throughout them all.

Chapter 13

When I went to bed that night, I considered never getting out of it for the rest of my life. The thought of having to go to school on Tuesday absolutely destroyed me. I didn't know how I could face anyone.

My parents had been really nice about taking me straight home after I'd finally left the ladies' room. They hadn't asked me questions, either, just told me they were around if I wanted to talk to them about things. But there was nothing really to talk about. Jessica didn't like me, never had and never would. And if Libby ever had liked me, she didn't anymore. Michelle and Amy might, but they were Jessica's friends first, and I was sure they wouldn't want to do anything with me if Jessica didn't. And Jessica never would again.

I couldn't even turn to Mary Kay for comfort. I couldn't remember a time when

Mary Kay wasn't on my side, and now she was mad at me too. And if I remembered correctly, she had every right to be mad. I hadn't been calling her, I hadn't been paying attention to her. I'd just been worrying that she might seem too babyish for Jessica and her friends. I had a horrible sickening feeling that I was the one who'd been babyish all the time. Me with all my talk about being such a sophisticated friend. I wasn't sophisticated, and I sure wasn't a friend. There was a real good chance I was the awfullest person in the world, and deserved to feel as miserable as I did.

Sunday morning I made a quick trip to the bathroom and then ran back to my room and closed the door. I figured my parents would keep busy fussing over Paul for a while, and they probably wouldn't even notice I was missing. In two or three days they might start worrying, but by then I'd have come down with some awful disease and never be able to get out of bed again. I wished I had the medical dictionary in my room so I could pick which awful disease it would be. Without it, I'd just have to be surprised.

"Come on out! Cathy, come on! I need to talk to everybody! Come on, don't be a stinkbomb!"

Even in a coma, I would have heard that. Andrea was back and pounding on my door.

"Go away," I muttered and buried my head in my pillow. There was no way I could deal with Andrea just then. With my luck, she'd prepared us a fabulous Sunday brunch of anchovies in cherry sauce and expected all of us to try it on the spot.

"Come on out, pumpkin," Andrea pleaded. "I have really important news, and I want you to hear it with everybody else."

"Good news?" I asked suspiciously.

"Great news," she replied.

The last thing I wanted to hear was any-body else's good news. But Andrea had been really nice to me except for her cooking, and I guessed I owed her. "I'll be right down," I said. "I want to get dressed first."

"Make it fast," Andrea said. "I'm burst-ing with my news."

"Okay," I grumbled. I got out of bed, but I didn't make it, in case I wanted to crawl back in it in a hurry. I threw on a shirt and my jeans and paddled downstairs barefoot. There was only so much I was willing to do for Andrea's good news.

"I'm glad you're all here," Andrea said as we gathered around her in the living room. "I wish Mark were here too. I guess I'll call him later to tell him."

"Tell him what, dear?" Mom asked.

"Yeah, could you speed it up?" Paul asked. "I've got things to do."

"The most amazing thing happened yesterday," Andrea said. "As you know, I went to my friend Dorrie's wedding."

"It seems to me I remember something about that," Dad said. Paul gave him a dirty look.

"Well, Dorrie and I have a lot of mutual friends," Andrea said. "After all, we did go to college together. And one of the other guests was a former mutual friend named Harvey."

"Not that creep Harvey?" I asked, rousing myself from my severe depression long enough to ask.

"Don't call him that," Andrea said. "He's changed. We talked and talked, and I can honestly say that my splitting up with him was the best thing that has ever happened to him."

"I never doubted it," Paul said.

Andrea glanced in his direction. "It mellowed him," she continued. "It made him examine his priorities, and made him realize how important our relationship was to him. It made him realize that if the two of us are to have a future, he's going to have to change."

"I didn't realize the two of you had a future," Mom said. "I really thought you'd split up with him for good."

"That's what I thought too," Andrea replied. "In fact, I told Harvey that every time he called, but I guess he never believed me."

"I didn't know he'd been calling," Dad said.

"You didn't?" Andrea said, trying to sound cool. "Oh, that's right. He always called before five. Anyway, we're going to give it another shot. Not that we're getting married or anything."

"Thank God for small favors," Dad said. This time Mom shot the withering look.

"But we've decided we have to give the relationship another chance," Andrea said. "No strings, no commitments. Just take it one day at a time and see how how it goes."

"If you think that's a good idea, dear," Mom said.

"I know you need proof," Andrea said. "I needed proof too, that Harvey really has changed. Something more than phone calls and cookbooks. But Harvey had the proof for me, and I think it will convince you too."

"We're listening," Dad said. We all were too, even Paul.

"Harvey has bought a Burger Bliss franchise with the money from his grandmother's trust fund!" Andrea proclaimed. "He bought it just for me."

"Romance isn't dead," Dad said.

"This is more than romance," Andrea said. "Romance comes and goes. This is a gesture of respect for my culinary skills."

"Burger Bliss?" Mom asked. "I really don't understand, Andrea."

"This isn't going to be just any Burger Bliss," Andrea said. "Harvey and I talked about it all through the reception. We're going to merge the arts of nouvelle cuisine and fast foods. We're going to create new vistas, seek out new horizons for American cooking."

None of us had anything to say after that.

"Anyway, I'm moving back in with Harvey this weekend," Andrea said. "So Paul will have his dance floor back, and you can get the TV set out of the living room, and you can all go back to your bad eating habits, and Dad can regain the ten pounds he's lost. I'm sure that'll make you all very happy."

"No!" I cried. "I don't want you to go!"

"Oh, pumpkin," Andrea said, and she ran over to me and hugged me. "I won't be far, just in Boston. I'll be home for Thanksgiving. And you can come visit me anytime you want."

"It isn't fair!" I cried, and ran out of the room. I set a new record for getting to my bedroom and slamming my door. I'd just lost Jessica and Libby and Mary Kay, and I'd already lost Francie and Mark, and now I had to lose Andrea too. I jumped onto my bed and hid under my blankets. Nothing or no one was ever going to make me get out from under them again.

At least no one knocked on my door. They left me alone, which was all I wanted. My world kept coming to an end, and I wanted to be alone forever to sob.

Forever lasted about an hour. There was a knock on my door, and my mother peeked her head in.

"Do you want to talk about it?" she asked me.

I shook my head. "Go away," I said.

"You should talk to somebody," she said. "Isn't there somebody you think would understand?"

I shook my head again.

"Come on, honey," Mom continued. "How about Mark? Would you feel better if you talked to him? Andrea wants to call him anyway, so you could talk to him first if you want."

I thought about it. Sometimes I thought that the person I missed most was Mark. And he always did understand me, even when no one else did.

"Can I talk to him first?" I asked. "Alone, no one else on the phone?"

"You sure can," Mom said. "Andrea wants to tell him about Harvey, and Paul wants to tell him about the dance recital. So we'll let each one of you have a few minutes on the phone with him alone. You can go first."

"Okay," I said and wiped the tears off my face. Mom smiled at me and left the door open. I heard her go into her bedroom and dial the number. In a moment or two she called my name, and I went to the bedroom and took the phone from her.

"Hi, Cathy," Mark said. "What's happening?"

So I started crying again. I felt really dumb crying long-distance like that, but it felt so good to hear his voice.

"It's okay, Cath," he said. "Just tell me what's the matter."

"I don't have any friends!" I sobbed. But then I swallowed back the tears and managed to tell him a little bit about Jessica and Libby and Mary Kay and the awful mess I was in.

"If Jessica doesn't like you that's her loss," Mark said. "You're a terrific person, Cathy, and Jessica sounds like a real turkey not to realize it."

"Oh, no," I said. "It's me, not her."

"No," Mark said. "It's her, not you, and don't you forget it. Besides, she sounds a little weird to me, living in that spotless house and always being polite to grown-ups. Are you sure she's really an earthling?"

I almost giggled.

"Mary Kay is an old friend of yours, though," Mark continued. "And I remember liking Libby way back when you were friends."

"I think I really hurt both of them," I said.

"I think you did too," Mark said. "And I think you should apologize to them. It's amazing what an apology can do for friends."

"You think they'll forgive me?" I asked.

"It's worth a shot," Mark said. "What do you have to lose?"

"Nothing," I admitted. I had nothing left to lose.

"Good," Mark said. "Talk to both of

them, and get things straightened out. And then write to me and tell me how it went. I want to know, Cathy. I love you, and I want to know how things are going with you. Don't you ever forget that."

I thought I might start crying again, so I just sort of gulped out "goodbye" and ran out of the room. "I'm off the phone," I shouted and sure enough in a moment I heard Paul's voice describing the dance recital to Mark.

I waited impatiently for the sound of the phone being hung up, and when it was, I made a quick grab for it. Who knew how many phone calls everybody else wanted to make? But none of their calls could be quite as important as mine.

The first call was to Mary Kay because I'd known her longer, and she scared me less. I wouldn't even let myself think about the possibility that she wasn't home.

I didn't have to worry about that. She answered the phone herself.

"It's Cathy," I said real fast. "And you were right yesterday. I have been neglecting you, and I'm real sorry."

"What made you figure that out?" she asked.

"Oh, Mary Kay," I said with a sigh. "Isn't it enough that I'm calling to apologize?"

"No," she replied. "You've been really awful lately, and I want to know what's been going on."

"Come on over for supper tonight," I said. "I promise you I'll tell you everything then."

"It had better be good," she said.

"It isn't," I said. "It isn't good at all. But I'm counting on you to understand."

"Okay," she said. "Will Libby be over too? I enjoyed seeing her that time."

"I don't know yet," I said. "I hadn't thought to ask her."

"Well, either way is okay with me," Mary Kay said. "I'll see you tonight, Cathy. And I'm glad you're becoming a human being again."

"I'm glad too," I said and we hung up. It was wonderful having a friend like Mary Kay, who understood things and forgave you anyway. I just hoped Libby would turn out to be that sort of friend too.

I thought about calling her while I still had control of the phone, but I realized that was the cowardly thing to do. I owed Libby a visit in person. She had the right to scream at me to my face. So I put the phone down, ran to my room to put on socks and sneakers, then went downstairs, and got my jacket. It was a pretty autumn day, with the leaves turning, and the

164

mums still in full flower. Definitely not the sort of day to be miserable. I hoped Libby would realize that and agree to make up with me.

I almost ran out of nerve when I reached Libby's house, and it took me a minute before I could ring her bell. But I did, and soon Mrs. Katz opened the door.

"Hi, Cathy," she said. "Come on in. I'm glad to see you."

"Hi," I said, wishing I were a million miles away.

"I don't know what's going on with Libby, but it must be pretty bad," Mrs. Katz said. "She's in her room. Maybe it would help if you talked with her."

"I'll try," I whispered. Mrs. Katz smiled at me, and I left the hallway and walked up the stairs to Libby's room. Her door was closed, and I knocked on it. "It's me, Cathy," I said. "Can I come in?"

"Okay," Libby said, so I opened the door. Libby was on her bed, looking as bad as I had on mine. I almost smiled to see her like that.

"I came to apologize," I said. "Can I sit down?"

"All right," Libby said, sitting up on her bed. I sat down on the chair near her desk.

"There was a mixup about the recital," I said. "A lot of it was my fault, but I don't think all of it was. But I wasn't honest with you about it, and I hurt your feelings and I want to apologize."

"What wasn't your fault?" Libby asked.

"I didn't ask Jessica to go," I said.

"You really expect me to believe that?" Libby asked. "The way you've been chasing after her all year?"

I shrank back. "Look, if you don't want to talk to me I can go," I said. "But I'm not going to listen to you say I'm lying when I'm not."

"Don't go," Libby said. "Please."

"Paul invited her," I said. "I didn't remember to ask him to hold the ticket for you just in case. I never even remembered to ask him for it in the first place. And he asked Jessica before you canceled. But then you didn't think you'd be going and I didn't think you'd ever find out. And I didn't think it was that great to go to the dumb recital anyway. But I should have told you that I'd forgotten and that he'd asked Jessica last week. Or I should have told Jessica yesterday that you'd be going instead. I haven't been real good at being honest lately with anybody, and I'm really sorry you don't trust me anymore."

"I sure want to trust you," Libby said. "I know you like Jessica more than you like me."

"She doesn't like me," I said. "And you're right, I have been chasing after her, and she doesn't like me. So I'm not going to like her anymore. It isn't worth it. Besides, I've always had more fun with you than with Jessica."

Libby smiled. "You don't think it's that easy, do you?" she asked. "You don't stop liking somebody like that."

"No, I guess not," I said, thinking about Andrea and Harvey. I'd have to tell Libby all about that when we got things back to normal. If we ever did.

"Anyway, I owe you an apology too," Libby said, squirming in her bed.

"You do?" I asked. It would be nice to be on that end of an "I'm sorry."

Libby looked down at the floor. "I knew you weren't invited to Jessica's sleepover," she said. "I mentioned it last night just to hurt you."

"Well, you sure succeeded," I replied.

"I was angry," Libby said sharply. "And I wanted to get back at you. I'm not a saint, Cathy. I've been trying and trying to get you to like me, and you kept chasing after Jessica instead and finally I saw you doing something with Jessica that I'd been hoping you would do with me, and it made me mad. I don't suppose you've ever been mad."

"Once or twice," I said. "But I try not to hurt people on purpose."

"You don't have to," Libby said. "You're so good at doing it by accident."

I stared at her horrified. But she looked so small and sad on her bed, and I knew she had a point. I had hurt her. So instead of running out of the room or screaming at her or wishing I was dead, I said "Truth or dare" to her.

"What's the dare?" Libby asked.

"I dare you to get out of bed and get dressed in one minute flat," I said. "It's a beautiful day, and if we're going to fight, we might as well do it outside."

"One minute?" Libby asked. "That's not much time."

"You can do it," I said. "On your mark, get set, go."

So Libby jumped out of bed, ran to her chest of drawers, grabbed some underwear, pulled off her pajamas and put on her underwear, ran to her closet, pulled down a shirt and slacks, and had the shirt half-buttoned when the minute ended.

"I win," I announced.

"I'm still going to get dressed," Libby said, and I watched while she did. "Okay, Cathy. Ask me anything and I'll tell you the truth."

"Do you think we can still be friends?" I asked, almost scared to look at her.

Libby tucked in her blouse and zipped up her pants. She turned around and faced me so I had to look up at her. "I think so," she said. "Probably, if it's really nice out."

"It's beautiful out," I said.

"Well, then," Libby said. "Let's go outside and see."

About the Author

SUSAN BETH PFEFFER is a native
New Yorker. She enjoys Emily Brontë,
baseball, and film (not necessarily in that
order), and has traveled to Tanzania. She
graduated from New York University with
a B.A. in Television, Motion Pictures, and
Radio. She has written many books for
young readers and young adults, including
Starting With Melodie and *Kid Power*
available as Apple paperbacks.